NICOLA BARKER's eight novels include *Darkmans* (short-
listed for the 2007 Man Booker and Ondaatie prizes, nd

short stories,
more than twenty lan

From the reviews of *Small Holdings*:

'This marvellous short novel explodes into action, with
Barker letting off fireworks and flares in all directions,
performing dazzling verbal gymnastics. She has a great
talent for the creation of eccentric characters, and the
assorted misfits in *Small Holdings* fizz with playfulness
and the author's obvious delight at her own powers of
invention. A hilarious and remarkably assured novel'
ALEX CLARK, *TLS*

'Funny and intelligent. Barker's sense of plot and comic
timing is faultless: she goes for big effects, which
resound brilliantly within the small space her narrative
describes, and holds the whole thing together with
writing that is resolved down to the last detail. *Small
Holdings* paints the big picture on a small canvas, cap-
turing in it the universality that is the essence of good
writing'   RACHEL CUSK, *The Times*

'Edgy and comic, it succeeds by virtue of Barker's
flamboyant sense of the absurd'   *Elle* magazine

By the same author

Love Your Enemies
Reversed Forecast
Heading Inland
Wide Open
Five Miles from Outer Hope
Behindlings
Clear
Darkmans
Burley Cross Postbox Theft

NICOLA BARKER

Small Holdings

FOURTH ESTATE • *London*

Fourth Estate
An imprint of HarperCollins*Publishers*
77–85 Fulham Palace Road
Hammersmith
London W6 8JB

This Fourth Estate paperback edition published 2011
1

First published in Great Britain by Faber and Faber Ltd 1995
Previously published in paperback by Faber and Faber Ltd 1996,
and by Flamingo in 2003

A catalogue record for this book is available from the British Library

ISBN 978-0-00-743604-0

Set in Palatino

Printed and bound in Great Britain by Clays Ltd, St Ives plc

Mixed Sources
Product group from well-managed
forests and other controlled sources
www.fsc.org Cert no. SW-COC-001806
© 1996 Forest Stewardship Council

FSC is a non-profit international organisation established to promote the
responsible management of the world's forests. Products carrying the FSC
label are independently certified to assure consumers that they come
from forests that are managed to meet the social, economic and
ecological needs of present and future generations.

Find out more about HarperCollins and the environment at
www.harpercollins.co.uk/green

Empty-handed I go, and behold the spade is in my hands;
I walk on foot, and yet on the back of an ox I am riding;
When I pass over the bridge,
Lo, the water floweth not, but the bridge doth flow.

Shan-hui

THREE DAYS

Wednesday
Thursday
Friday

Wednesday

SOME PEOPLE OPEN up like flowers; slowly, painstakingly, each petal unfurling, reacting, affirming. Responding, simply, to warmth and to tending.

Other people can be peeled; like a fruit – like an orange or a pomelo – the skin comes off, and underneath is something full and ripe, perfectly segmented, waiting to be apportioned by deft and inquisitive fingers.

Doug was like an egg. A boiled egg. Hard-boiled. He was knocked once, twice, many times, and his shell cracked, and it crumbled, and underneath was something slippery and rubbery and not especially digestible.

If he hadn't been hard-boiled, he would have dropped from his shell, moist, sloppy, just a mess. In certain respects, in retrospect, that might have been preferable.

I'd been wrong about Doug all along. I'd thought he was an oyster: barnacle-hard outside, abrasive even, but with a vulnerable interior, maybe a pearl in there somewhere, hidden, precious, protected. I also considered at certain points that he might be a beetle. Beetles, it seems, like some other insects, have a skeleton on the outside and the flesh, the soft bits, inside. People are traditionally soft on the outside, and the bones, the frame, the supports are hidden away within layers of skin and fat and muscle. That's exactly how I am. Soft and yielding, like tripe to the touch.

Well Doug, Doug was a boiled egg, hard-boiled with a blue-ish pallor – white turned blue – a pale yellow yolk (his heart, not soft either), and he was extremely entrenched, obscenely contained and mystifyingly, ridiculously, maybe even *deceptively* proud of himself.

We'd all worked as gardeners in the park for several years before the whole enterprise was privatized and a group of us – me, Doug and not forgetting Ray (Big Ray) – formed a partnership and along with Nancy, our driver, made a successful bid for the contract.

3

Doug was always nominally in charge. I'm too shy to do anything but blush and blunder. Ray, well, he's moonish, and tender and completely unfocused. Doug is incredibly reasonable, too reasonable – monosyllabic, in general, admittedly – awesome, though, terrifying, as hard as a nut; a literal toughnut. He is fair-minded but merciless. If he has a rule book (and he'll usually find one close at hand) then he'll play by it.

Working with Doug is like playing a game of snooker. The park is the green baize. We all look after the baize, we nurture it, we love it – but more of that later – and Doug is the white ball. He sets all the other balls in motion. He doesn't confer, he doesn't request, he doesn't even cooperate. Doug simply knocks into the other balls, slams into them, bangs into them. Balls of all colours. And I'm a red ball. Shy. Embarrassed. Always the first to be pocketed, to scamper and scarper.

Doug's technique is remarkably simple. Physical. He's the big ball, the biggest ball. That's all. He is also, and I guess this is ironic – or else this whole snooker business just isn't working – Doug is also the black ball. He is the first and the last. If he leaves the table then the game is over.

There's one question you should never ask Doug. Never ask Doug where he's from. I know where he's from because many is the time I've heard him talking French, a strange French, like a list of exotic ingredients from a fancy cookbook, to his wife, Mercy, who he walked out on a fortnight ago after thirty years of marriage.

Doug comes from a place full of bright birds and sun and tall trees. I can imagine this place so clearly, can even imagine Doug there, kicking up sand, shouting at people. It's an island. One island in the Lesser Antilles: Martinique. I looked it up in my big old atlas. I saw the arc of Doug's islands, islands humped in the Caribbean sea like the backbone of a long-forgotten animal. Barbuda, Antigua, Guadeloupe, Dominica, Martinique, St Lucia, St Vincent, Grenada, Doug's Islands.

Everything about him gives him away, external things, so he holds himself in, his real self, his inside-self, every-part.

Every muscle tenses, resists, contains. That's Doug all over. With his neat greying beard, his black hair, his hands like clams, his dark, bloodied eyes, his accent which is as strong and thick as rich molasses.

In fact, though, in truth, he comes from Palmers Green, North London. We all do: me and Ray and Doug and Saleem (one-legged Saleem, our squatter, my persecutor, our old curator) and Nancy. That Nancy.

Well, the park is my soul. I live off it, I work on it, I live for it. I love it. Doug loves it too, but lately he's taken to growing vegetables – out back, in the greenhouses which are no longer open to the public. Giant vegetables. He thinks the punters don't notice when they peek through the glass, expecting succulents, orchids, exotica. He thinks they aren't surprised, shocked, maybe even *piqued* when they see only row upon row of onions (Doug's an onion, yes, I like that. An onion) or marrows, cabbages, tomatoes. The occasional giant, merry sprig of a carrot top.

'Phil,' Doug said, last time I broached the subject of the vegetables – and the other things too, more recent peculiarities – 'Phil.' (He takes every opportunity to say my name, rolls it on his tongue, pronounces it 'feel', which never fails to activate something in me, something inside, something vulnerable and inadequate, something connected to feeling too much but expressing nothing, something soft and sad.) 'Phil, whosoever diggeth a pit shall fall in it.'

Doug has another saying, equally incomprehensible, which he'll interchange randomly with this one; 'Phil, Phil, what-ya gonna do when your well runs dry? Huh?' He won't wait for an answer. He's too preoccupied. He'll saunter off (that saunter, a true gardener's gait) and he'll be rubbing his hands, jangling the keys in his pocket and expectorating; drawing something deep from his throat which he'll expel neatly into the border as he wanders past the perennials.

By then I'll be blushing. Fool. I'm thinking about 'Feel'. *Feel*. Whosoever diggeth a pit.

5

Ray was digging a deep hole next to the perimeter fence on the east side of the park and preparing to sink a gate-post into it. He was glossy with sweat. He stopped digging as I approached.

'Whosoever diggeth a pit,' I said.

'Now that,' Ray answered mopping his wide forehead with his fat arm, 'That's Bobby Marley.'

'You're kidding me. I thought it was biblical.'

Ray shrugged. 'Could be originally, but I'm sure I heard it in a Bob Marley song.'

Ray must be well over twenty stone, has long, frizzy blonde hair, a straggly beard, green eyes, the face of a cherub. I told him Doug had requested a meeting at five, in the house, the kitchen.

'Fine.'

'You, me, him and Nancy.'

Ray rested on his spade. 'It seems like Doug's finally cracked,' he said, grinning gently. 'At long last. And that's what comes,' he added, 'that's what comes of being too solid for too long.'

I didn't like this kind of talk. 'He's only left his wife,' I said calmly. 'That's all.'

Ray remained undaunted. 'He's talking to himself.'

'I do that too, sometimes, when I'm not thinking clearly.'

'You're like royalty. You talk to your plants. Doug's just talking. All the time.'

'He's got a lot on his mind. There's the meeting with the council to re-assert our tender on Friday. That won't be much fun. It won't be easy. And Doug's the man to pull it off.'

Ray nodded his assent. 'Doug's the man, yes, but he hasn't done a stroke of work in weeks now.'

I shrugged. I said, 'He's keeping busy.'

Ray scowled. 'He's up to something,' he said. 'He's tipping the scales . . .'

Ray made a strange, scale-tipping gesture with his two arms. 'And I don't know,' he added, 'what that actually means for the rest of us, and for this place.'

6

He looked around him, at his spade, the mud, the grass, the fence.

I cleared my throat. I said, 'Things are chugging over, just like they've always done.'

Ray shrugged, yanked up his spade and returned to his digging. 'Someone,' he said, grunting out every syllable with each cut of the soil, 'Someone is going to have to do something.' And after he'd finished speaking, the slice of his spade added a further five syllables: *And it won't be me.*

I watched Ray digging for a moment. If only, I thought, Doug'd opened up gently, like a flower.

I had a thorough understanding of how flowers worked.

How big is it? Christ knows. An average size. Not a grand park. Not your Victoria, your Hyde, your Hampstead Heath. It seems small because of its unpretentiousness. Even so, it has pretensions. Used to have a Tudor museum – black, white, criss-crossed beams – stuck wham-bam in the middle of it, facing the water, reflected in the water; three little lakes and a round ornamental pond over to the right where kids paddle – contravening the park regulations – in the summer.

The museum was burned down, years ago now, but its black, burnt-out shell remains, and Saleem, its curator, well, more about her later. We used to have a proper athletics track: red, official, fenced off, very impressive, but we grew it over a while back. Athletes go down to Tottenham or up to Enfield now.

The tennis courts – six of them, slightly overgrown, but in working order – stand adjacent to the greenhouses. There's also a wild section, which is purposefully unkempt, circled by silver birch, where the squirrels dart. A bandstand, Doug's pride and joy, recently built at his instigation out of raw, dark-stained, splinter-pushing pine. An adventure playground that any park would be proud of.

To the north is the hill which is grass, mainly, where people come to picnic. We have public toilets – Ladies, Gents – and behind these are the private areas, staff-only places, which consist of a barn – a lovely barn – and the house where Saleem squats, where Doug is skulking, now he's left his wife. Now he's opened up and gone crackers.

It was three o'clock that same Wednesday afternoon and I was planting geraniums over by the bandstand. I had twenty plants in all and wasn't particularly optimistic about the contribution these would make to the display as a whole which was scruffy and sparse and relatively shambolic. This was Doug's patch, supposedly.

I was deciding whether to plant them in a half-moon, close to the border, or whether to distribute them more freely among the spider plants – this display's main constituent. The spider plants had been Ray's idea. His reasoning was that they grew quickly, reproduced easily, and that they were, most importantly, green. I doubted whether they'd last the winter out, but they'd cost us nothing which, as we're broke, was all that really mattered.

Nancy had promised to drive over a new, cheap assortment of annuals from Southend at some point. She'd arranged to get them on credit. She has the gift of the gab, and it's a useful gift. I wish I had it.

I dug a hole with my trowel near to the front of the bed. Behind me, as I worked, I could hear the gravel shift and scuffle, and another familiar noise, a plunging, a sucking-plucking. *One-legged Saleem*. I could see her from the corner of my eye, swinging over, staggering over. I pretended to be engrossed.

'Phil,' she said, 'what's up?' She drew very close. 'Planting pansies, eh?'

'Geraniums.' I popped one in and pressed the soil firm around its roots.

'Yeah? What's a geranium do?' She poked her stick out, automatically, and pushed it into the soft soil to the right of the new plant. 'How's that?'

'Thanks.'

I widened the hole with the trowel and placed the new plant.

8

'What's it do? I love knowing what they do. You're clever like that.'

'You could dry the root. It's astringent. A kind of tonic. You could take it internally for diarrhoea or use it as a gargle. It's a good gargle.'

'Who'd've thought it?' She bounced a step back and made a further hole. I moved over and planted the next one. 'Who'd've thought it, eh?'

I grimaced. She stared at me closely, 'Are you busy, Phil? Are you working too hard? Are you hot? Catching the sun, maybe? You've got bright little flames in both cheeks.'

I tried to distract her, to evade her questions, to drag her eyes away from my skin which always ripens at her approach, always reddens. 'You're getting mud on your stick.'

'Huh?' She inspected it, 'Nah, Soil's dry. Needs a water.'

'It's moist for August.'

'It's moist for August!'

She guffawed and threw herself down on to the grass verge. I glanced at her for a moment and then turned my back and carried on planting.

Saleem has long, black hair and a lean face. Skin the colour of caramel. Half dark Hindu, half Greek. A curious hybrid. She looks like a cobra in a wig. She speaks with a forked tongue. She hates me. I don't know why.

'Can we talk, Phil?'

'I'm working.'

'While you work, then.'

I smell her hate, always, and it's a hot-hate, has a hot smell which makes me shrivel, inside, outside. And she loves to stare, to invade, to gouge. She lives for it.

'While you work, then,' she repeated.

I said nothing.

'Am I irritating you or something?'

'No.'

She prodded the base of my back with the tip of her stick.

'Stop that.'

I swatted her stick with my arm but didn't turn.

9

'You're just too sensitive,' Saleem said, and by the sound of her voice she had a smile on her lips. 'And usually,' she added, 'I wouldn't care, but lately, well, things are coming to a head and I'm looking to you for some kind of decisive action.'

I didn't respond to this, didn't rise to her, and she, in turn, was silent for a minute, sitting up straight, viper-still, her amputated leg jutting out in front of her like the short butt of a cigar.

'You know, sometimes, Phil, your natural reserve comes across like a kind of hostility. Turn and look at me, Phil,' she added, almost whispering. 'Turn and look, go on. Go on, Phil. Turn and face me. Look at me. Go on.'

'I'm busy.'

My head was so low as I spoke that my chin touched my chest. She laughed at this. Her incisors are protrusive, are very clearly pointed. I could picture them in my mind, and the very idea of them scorched me, scalded me. She prodded me again, sharp in the back with her stick. 'Go on, Phil, go on. Go on.'

And I blocked out her taunting, was working, like I'd said, was busy, was working, was planting, was digging. Quickly, busily. Five plants, then four plants. Then three plants left, only three, and after I'd placed those I'd have to turn to face her and she'd see, with glee, that I was burned by her proximity, that I was red as beet, purple-red as beet. Two plants left. One plant.

I turned. But Saleem wasn't looking at me. She was a hooded reptile, yes, still a reptile, drawn up to spit, rocking, readying herself, but suddenly not focusing on me, but staring beyond me, over my shoulder, at the museum, its black shell. I thanked God for it, the museum. That was a skin she'd shed a long time ago, but she kept on inspecting it, sniffing at it, mulling it over.

I turned away again, shuffled the soil into smoothness with my palms, broke down lumps with my thumb and forefinger, patted it, softened it. And for a minute or so I was still blushing, red and ripe and bright as a poppy. Blood. My curse.

10

You see, I blushed before I could walk, before I could talk. People's eyes invade me and make me anxious. Maybe because I think too well of other people, or maybe because I don't think well enough of myself. My schooldays were tortured, my teenyears a wash-out, and when I grew older, my only recourse was to disguise. Girls wear green-tinted make-up. Yes, that helps to hide blushes, apparently. I grew my hair, a mass of curls that fall over my face, cover my ears, which always tingle first, sting and heat up. A neat and moderately well-spread beard – up my cheeks, down my neck – helps to shelter further exposed flesh. I am Monkey Man. I am Mountain Man. I am Scott of the Antarctic after a very long expedition.

Doug told me once, in a lighter moment, that my face was a vagina – all curls, all hair, with pink lips protruding and a small nose, labia-like, just above – a tender fold. After that I knew I didn't just feel strange, vulnerable, like a whelk when its shell has been jerked open, but that I seemed strange to others, that I looked strange to others.

It's all so complete, so perfect. A sun, a moon, a circle, a cycle. Maybe I think too much. Maybe I don't think enough. Saleem knows all this. She smells it. She sees it with her yellow eyes.

'What's that?' she asked suddenly, pointing with her stick. I followed its line. To the right of the museum I could see Doug in the distance, carrying what looked like a small tree.

'Doug.'

'What's he up to?'

'I don't know. He's working.'

'Come off it! Anyway. I don't mean Doug. I mean *that* . . .' She continued pointing and added, 'A plant. Inside the building, the museum.'

I squinted. It was too far to see anything, not clearly.

'It's a plant,' she insisted, 'crawling up where the chimney used to be.'

I looked again, still not seeing but vaguely remembering – the park, its constituent parts, every small thing etched in my very heart – I said, 'I think it's a passion flower, growing up in the charcoal and old cinder.'

'What kind of a plant?'

'A creeper. It has a beautiful flower. White and very ornate. In Jamaica they have a variation which they call a grenadilla. Doug might know more about it.'

'I bet it grew from my leg,' she said. 'My skin and foot. During the fire, that's where the burning beam fell, right there.'

I stared at her. She was warped. She was rubbing the stump of her knee, smiling. I shuddered.

'What does it do?'

'It works like a kind of morphine, affects the circulation and increases the rate of respiration. In homeopathic medicine they use its narcotic properties to treat dysentery. Sleeplessness. Some types are used for treating hysteria and skin inflammation.'

'Yeah? How?'

'I'm not sure. Dry the berry or boil the root. Something like that.'

Saleem started drawing a pattern in the grey gravel of the path with her stick.

'Let me tell you something, Phil,' she said. 'I was talking to Doug this morning, over breakfast. And guess what we talked about?'

I didn't turn but I shook my head.

'We talked about the Gaps.'

I carried on smoothing the soil, thinking of softness, soil-softness.

'Are you listening, Phil? The Gaps. Does that mean anything to you?'

I said quietly, 'It doesn't mean anything.'

'What was that?'

Saleem. My tormentor. I turned. 'I don't know.'

'OK,' she said, 'OK, so Doug has this theory, right, about why London doesn't work. It's to do with the postal districts. He has this theory about London not working . . . Did he tell you this yet?'

I shook my head.

'Oh, you'll love it. You'll love this. Here's how it goes: Doug says that everything in nature moves in a circle, OK? That's how nature works, a kind of winter–spring–summer–autumn–winter thing. A kind of sun-follows-moon-and-earth-revolving thing. Sort of oriental. He's into all this stuff lately. Anyhow, Doug has now decided that the city of London is a life form too, kind of like a complex bacteria, and as such, everything should fit together. But *unfortunately* . . .' She stressed this word until it stang with venom. 'Unfortunately, Phil, London can't work properly because of the Gaps. Sounding familiar yet?' I shook my head, although suddenly, strangely, it did begin to sound familiar. Doug. Circles. Doug. The Gaps. It did sound familiar.

In the gravel Saleem had drawn a circle. 'That's London,' she said, completing it. She drew a horizontal line through the centre of the circle, cutting it in half. 'And that's the Thames,' she added. 'So that's London and everything connects to everything else. And these are the postal districts, OK?' She drew them in. 'We've got plain North London, we've got plain West London, we've got plain East London . . .' As she spoke she pointed, and I could hear the gravel kissing and knocking.

'But here's a problem, right. There's South-West London postal districts and there's South-East postal districts, and they, sort of, meet in the middle, which means that there's no South. No plain South. And Doug's upset about this. And there's another problem too, right. There's North-West and South-West and South-East, but there's no North-East. Another Gap. No plain South and no North-East. And according to Doug, this is why London doesn't connect. This is why London doesn't work. Things aren't properly linked. See what I'm getting at, Phil?'

I nodded.

'You see, the city is *fucked*, Phil, because of this little problem with the postal districts. And Doug is worrying about it, Phil. He's thinking about it. These Gaps.'

I stopped feeling the soil. I turned.

'So what's the problem? Why are you telling me this?'

Saleem's eyes popped. 'Because Doug's going absolutely fucking crazy. He's got this meeting on Friday. Our whole fucking future depends on it, and he is going crazy. He's crazy.'

I turned away again.

'Say something!'

'He'll be fine.'

'No he won't be fine. And that's the worst part of it. You seem determined to ignore what's going on right under your nose. He's gone mad. I know all about it. I'm living in the same house as him. And no one asked me, incidentally, whether I minded or not. He just moved in and that was that. Anyhow, I can see my way around the whole thing but no one wants to know what I've seen.'

Saleem scratched out her Postal District London and prepared the gravel for another design: a large phallus. Medieval. A two-foot phallus pointing west to her north and east to my south. Pointing, I decided, towards Ray, far away, digging his pit.

'Doug's OK.'

'OK? Jesus! You don't know anything,' she said, slitting her eyes, angry now, 'You're so *in* on yourself. There's stuff going on here that you don't know anything about. Private stuff. Everything's a secret with Doug. You don't know about Mercy and the diarrhoea. You don't know about that mad man, that Chinaman, slinking about the place, poisoning everything. You don't see anything through all that fucking hair. You don't see *anything*.'

Saleem pushed herself up, used her stick to pull herself up by. She works well without her leg, admittedly, is lithe when she wants to be.

'And the thing is, she said, 'I know you love this place. It matters to you. You depend on it the same way I do. But you won't ever *act*, you won't ever *do* anything. You're *dormant*, just blind. Turning in on yourself.'

I was surprised to be connected, all of a sudden, in a rush, like this, with Saleem. It was a curious sensation, this connection.

'Forget it, then,' she said, sounding defeated and afterwards, almost instantly, sounding defiant. 'Looks like I'm going to have to be the one,' she muttered, turning her back, 'Me. Saleem. I am the one who'll have to save things. Ray's too stupid. You're just a yak, a blob. And Nancy . . .' She laughed. 'I am the one,' she said, darkly, stalking off, 'just watch me.'

SO THIS IS the problem, I told the exhaust on the back of Nancy's truck. The Park's got another four months to run and we're almost broke. On Friday Doug's going to meet Enfield Council's Park Management Committee to re-assert our tender.

Doug's been cryptic about his intentions. He's said he has plans, big plans, but he hasn't discussed them with me or Ray, he hasn't told us what he's up to. Saleem thinks that he doesn't care any more, that he's losing it, that he's liable to do just about anything. Now he's left his wife. Now he's left his home. I can't help thinking, though, somehow, that Doug's just like me, that he cares too much. But there's no telling, not with Doug. Doug won't tell. His lips are zipped. Like Saleem says, he's private. He's impenetrable.

And of course we're all frightened of him, apart from Saleem. Maybe even Saleem. He's getting bigger and bigger. Sometimes I glance at his eyes and see the whole world in there, streaming in – light and colour and nature and history. God only knows what he might do.

My one compensation is that at least I think I know what he's capable of. I know the perimeters. There are none.

And I love Doug for that very reason. I see my own smallness reflected in his hugeness, and because we are opposite we are almost the same.

I'm thirty-four years old and I can't even hold a conversation. I'm soggy and I'm limpid and I've never truly believed in anything but the things that I do. My work, this park. And I like plants. I can make them grow, and I like the sky, how it goes up and up with no lid, and I've never even kissed a girl. And I'm in love with Nancy.

At least I think I am, and for all the wrong reasons. I love Nancy because she never looks me in the eye. That's her way. She's too preoccupied. There's something in her gaze that doesn't focus, doesn't invade. I am only a voice in her head, so I'm safe, it's a safe love. You see, she isn't like other girls.

Nancy's our driver. She has two great passions in her life: to drive her truck and the truck itself. (A Leyland Daf Roadrunner, 'Truck of the Year,' she tells me proudly, 'when it first came out.' Seven tons of silver and metal and diesel.)

Also, Nancy likes to run. She has a body like a wasp; so clean so neat, so sharp. She can be very mean, potentially, but she often chooses not to be. She's a man-woman, an Amazon, an outlaw. She has a small, silver pistol in her truck, in the glove compartment, smokes slim cheroots, wears denim jeans ripped off above the knee, and her muscles, smooth like cream, leg muscles, arm muscles, a tan, darker down one side of her body and face, a driving tan.

In summer she'll wear a short leather halter-top. Her small breasts, like two beige damsons, jutting up, vibrating as she pulls the truck in, struggling in low gear, still when the engine's off. She's a reconstructed Suzi Quatro, a Joan Jett of jammed-up junctions. Sticky and tricky.

She is strong. She moves the load, effortlessly, at speed. She likes picking people up, can even pick Ray up, can do basic judo, play football, baseball, basketball. Has broken both arms, both legs, her collar bone in motorbike accidents. She told me so, she did.

She is covered, like a cactus, in tiny blonde hairs: her face, her arms, her legs. And the light shines off her, and the sweat, when she's hot (always hot), beads on her and transforms her body into a silken web, so ornate, wondrous, one of the wonders of the world, in the world, out of this very, very world.

Nancy.

Nancy switched off her engine.

'I'm fucked,' she said, staring past my ear and into the middle distance. 'My side-light's gone. I'm gonna have to tell Doug. He'll blow.'

'What happened?'

'I dunno. Some guy pulled out and I didn't see him. Halfway to Southend. I was too uptight, too stressed. Just

17

stupid. It's been churning in my stomach all the way home.
Third claim in two months. Here's the paper,' she slung me a
copy of the *Guardian*, 'that's all they had left at the services.'

'Anything in it?'

'Nah.'

I rolled up the paper and stuck it in my back pocket, then
said, 'We're having a meeting in a minute, in the kitchen.
D'you need a hand unloading?'

'Nope. I'll be fine. Better start without me.'

'Why?'

'Doug'll blow when I tell him about the bump I had. I can't
face it right now.'

'D'you want me to tell him?'

She climbed out of her cab. 'Would you? If the moment's
right? If he's in a good mood. Don't mention it otherwise.'

'Fine.'

'Would you?'

'Sure.'

'Thanks. You're a gem.'

She rolled up her sleeves and went to let down the truck's
tail.

Ray was in the kitchen devouring a packet of ginger-nuts. He
offered me the packet.

'No thanks. Seen Doug?'

'He's on the phone.'

I started preparing a pot of tea. Saleem appeared in the
doorway, 'That's fine, Ray, those are mine but just help
yourself.'

'Sorry.' He put down the biscuits and furtively brushed
some crumbs from his beard.

'Let me do that.' Saleem pushed past me and picked up the
teapot, took off the lid and peered inside. 'Doug never rinses
this properly.'

I took the paper from my pocket, opened it, held it high and
started turning the pages. On the third page, in the Reuters
column, two small items had been outlined in blue ink. I

peered more closely at them. The first had the heading THUMB SALAD. It said:

A nurse who found the tip of a thumb in a take-away salad was awarded £200 compensation. Rebecca Pothecary, who bought the food from Anthony's Take-Away on Tottenham Street, central London, 'felt something resist her bite', Clerkenwell magistrates were told. The sandwich bar was ordered to pay £600 in fines and costs for breaching health regulations.

Outside my paper-wall I could hear Ray reaching quietly again, gently, for the ginger-nuts; the crackle of the packet, his fingers prodding inside, his nail catching the rim of a biscuit and easing it out. Saleem had her back to him, engrossed in the task of filling the kettle, fitting on its lid. I heard the water slosh inside it.

The second item in the paper, underlined, directly below the first, had the headline, 100-DAY PROTEST. It said:

Peter Hawes yesterday spent his 100th day welded inside his roadside café. Mr Hawes, 48, is fighting a government decision to close down the lay-by at Guyhirn in Cambridgeshire, where he has cooked for travellers for years.

Ray had the ginger-nut between his teeth now, bit down softly. I heard the sugar snap and then an unobtrusive crunching, a short silence, another snap, more crunching. Saleem pushed the kettle's plug into the wall and then turned on the power switch. I waited to hear the water in the kettle starting to gurgle, I waited for Saleem to notice Ray's chewing, I waited for Ray to gag and swallow, but all I heard, suddenly, was silence, like each sound had been extracted, sucked out, expunged. I tried to turn a page of my paper but it didn't move. My eyes focused in front of me, on the words *felt something resist her bite*, the words *felt something resist*, the words *felt . . . resist* the word *felt felt . . . felt*. Doug was standing in the doorway. Doug was standing next to me.

'Phil.'

19

Feel. All the sounds returned in a rush. At once. Doug was standing there and he was smaller than I'd remembered and he had his hands in his pockets and he was smiling.

'If this is our meeting,' Doug said, 'our business meeting, then what is she doing in here?'

Doug tipped his head towards Saleem. Saleem bridled, 'Aren't I even allowed in my own kitchen now?'

Doug continued to smile. 'This is not your kitchen, Saleem. It is our kitchen. This house belongs to the business. You used to work here, yes. You used to have some right to live in this place. When you were a curator. But now the museum is gone, you have no function. You stay here on sufferance, you have stayed here for years, on sufferance, because you have one leg and you lost the other one in a fire, and I feel sorry for you and Ray feels sorry for you and Phil, too, feels sorry for you. But this is not your kitchen. This is our kitchen and we let you borrow it. And you should remember that fact. Now would you get out, please.'

'Fuck you, Doug,' Saleem said, calmly. 'D'you know what a grenadilla is?' she asked, not sounding in the least bit ruffled.

'I know what a grenadilla is, yes.'

'I gave my own flesh for this place,' she whispered. 'What can you give?'

Doug said nothing. He watched her and then he said, 'Go away.'

Saleem laughed. I moved the paper up closer to my face as she swung past me. 'And what're you doing?' she asked, saucily. 'Eating that thing?' Close up she smelled like a bunch of watercress. A peppery smell. I folded the paper, my face tingling. 'If you don't mind,' she added, 'I'll borrow that.'

She snatched the paper and swung out.

Doug filled the kitchen. Ray's fatter – twice as fat – and I'm big enough and hairy enough, but Doug has personality. Doug has backbone, is a true vertebrate. Ray and I are rheumy, watery creatures that ride the waves but Doug's already clambered on shore.

'Where's Nancy?' Doug asked.

'I dunno. Phil?' Ray looked to me.

'Outside. Unloading.'

Doug leaned against the sink. 'Nancy's got to go,' he said, 'I just got a call from our insurance. She had another accident this morning. Almost killed two people. Her fault.'

Ray and I stared at each other.

'We can't afford the insurance premiums any more,' Doug said. 'They keep on going up and up. It's out of control. We've got to tidy this stuff away. Nothing will work until we tidy this stuff away. That's all I'm saying.'

'And just hear this,' he added, warming to his subject now. 'She only went and contacted the insurance people from the services on her way back and said she'd pay the difference herself and something extra if they didn't tell us. If they didn't tell me. That's what the man just told me on the phone.'

'I can't see why she shouldn't do that,' Ray said, boldly.

Doug ignored this, 'She wouldn't even have mentioned it, not a word, not a single word.'

I almost said something, but when I opened my mouth I was only coughing.

'That's deception,' Doug said. 'We can't trust her. She's a liability.'

'I like her,' Ray said cheerfully. 'She's OK.'

Doug focused on Ray. 'Ray,' he said, 'you have all the business sense of a Savoy cabbage.'

Ray smiled. 'True,' he said, 'I see your point, Doug.'

After a short pause, I said, 'I think we should wait a while before we make any decisions. Give it some thought. Take a vote, later on. And maybe we should think about the meeting on Friday before all this other business.'

'It's under control,' Doug said, haughty. 'I want Nancy out. I can't operate, I can't deal with that kind of deception. I'll tell her to her face when she crawls in here. No problem.'

'It's just . . .' I said, 'It's only . . .'

'First things first, Phil,' Doug said, calmly. 'We'll lance her like a boil. Tidy things up a bit.'

Ray's face began to move, to curdle, like he was having a

thought which was germinating in his big, fat cheeks, swelling, expanding, filling him up.

'Doug,' he said, his thought at last finding a voice, a small voice, 'Doug, we were all thinking that maybe you should take things a bit easy for a while . . .'

Doug stared calmly at Ray, his eyes taking in Ray's pink lips and his yellow beard, his several chins, the dimple in his cheek.

'You're going crazy, fat boy, you're crazy if you think I need to take things slow. I'm only just starting. I'm taking stock, fat boy. I'm seeing things big and I'm seeing them better than I've ever seen them. Better than ever.'

Ray looked at his hands. Ten fingers, all in good working order. 'Uh, fine,' he said. 'It's just that Phil . . .'

Doug turned, 'Phil?'

I scratched my neck, my brain fizzy and empty. The kitchen is only a small room and it hasn't been decorated in years. Above the oven, grease has stained the wallpaper a steamy yellow. The grey floor tiles are full of prints, footprints and mud-prints and cat-prints.

'Is there something you're wanting to say to me Phil? Anything? The meeting on Friday? Anything you think I can't handle? Want to tell me?'

It's not exactly that I *couldn't* say anything, more that I didn't really have anything *to* say. What was my evidence, after all? Doug was being strange, but thinking about it, he'd always been irascible, changeable, unpredictable. It wasn't so much anything in particular, any special fact or detail I was burdened with, more a feeling, a sensation.

Saleem had said that we were connected in some way, she and I, the two of us, connected together, against Doug, because Doug was thinking about Gaps, and thinking about making Gaps. And Nancy . . . and Nancy . . . And I was contemplating all these things when I suddenly heard a voice and the voice was saying, 'I love this place, Doug. I love this place.' It was my voice. Blood rushed into my cheeks. I felt a stabbing sensation in my chest.

Doug's face broke into a broad grin. His teeth were tombstones.

'Phil,' he said, laughing, 'I'm going to the greenhouse. Gonna have a little talk to my big vegetables.'

And off he went.

As soon as Doug had gone, Saleem bounced back in. She put her stick down on the table, pulled out a chair and sat down.

'Now what? Nancy's in some kind of trouble?'

Ray nodded. His expression was so mournful and forlorn that it looked like his cheeks were in danger of melting and dripping and dribbling down on to the table. 'Oh God,' he said, 'her timing's less than perfect.' I couldn't think of anything to add. Eventually I said, 'Let's not get this all out of proportion.'

'No?' Ray glanced up, hopeful, 'You think it'll work itself out?'

'More than likely.'

'Oh shut up, Phil,' Saleem snapped. 'What the fuck do you know?'

My skin felt tight. I looked at my watch, 'It's nearly time to knock off.'

'I need a drink,' Ray said, 'and a few packets of crisps. Want to come to The Fox for a while?'

Before I could answer the kitchen door opened slightly and Cog wandered in. Cog was the park's cat who behaved like a dog, was dogged and doggish, ran for sticks and didn't mind a cuff and a wrestle. Nancy was two paces behind him.

'Me and Cog are going for a run together,' she announced. Her voice was just a fraction too loud.

'Did you see Doug?' Ray asked nervously.

'Doug? I saw him.'

She walked to the sink and rinsed her hands. She seemed calm.

'Did Doug say anything?' Ray asked, even more nervously.

'Doug says a lot of things, Doug's a sandwich short of a picnic.'

23

'Doug's elevator,' Ray grinned, 'doesn't stop at all floors.'

'That's as maybe,' I said, 'but above all else, it's Doug who holds this place together.'

Saleem cocked her head at this. 'I don't think so,' she said. 'It's you that holds this place together, and Ray, and even Nancy. Doug holds the business together.'

'It's the same thing,' I said, confident of this fact.

'Not at all.'

Nancy dried her hands on a tea towel. 'I'm going for a run,' she said, 'Come on, Cog.' She slapped her thigh. Cog came to heel.

'Didn't Doug say anything?' Ray asked, for the second time. Nancy started jogging gently on the spot, warming up. 'Did Phil tell you,' she asked Ray, still very loud, 'that I had another knock in the truck?'

Saleem intervened on my behalf. She said, 'Doug already knew. The insurance people rang him.'

'I was unloading the privet from the van,' Nancy said, 'and Doug came over and asked me to load it up again.'

Saleem, I noticed, was watching Nancy closely, staring at her, and she had a smile on her lips but her eyes were full of something else, an intensity, a fixity, a cruelty.

'Privet?' I asked, unable to stop myself. 'You were unloading privet?'

Nancy nodded, distracted. 'Neat bushes with small, dark green leaves. A ton of them.'

'You don't need to tell Phil what privet is,' Ray said, smiling glumly. 'He's the Plant King.'

'Come off it.' My cheeks tightened a fraction more and I started to glow.

'Yeah, well,' Nancy tucked her T-shirt into her running shorts. 'I'm going for a run,' she said, and before anyone could respond, she'd slammed her way out and sprinted off.

Saleem turned to me. 'He's gone and sacked her,' she said. 'So what are you two going to do about it?'

Ray stared towards the door, after Nancy, his expression inscrutable.

'Let's just sit this one out,' I said. 'Doug won't actually get rid of Nancy. He's just letting off steam.'

'I don't know.' Ray looked uncertain. 'I mean, I like Nancy and I respect Doug. I like them both. But they've both done things and they've both said things . . . I dunno.' Ray picked up the packet of ginger-nuts and ate another one.

'What's Nancy said?' Saleem asked, suddenly sounding interested. I turned too, focused on Ray, slightly daunted by his apparent overview.

'Huh?' Ray stopped chewing.

'What kind of things?' Saleem persisted.

'Stuff.'

Saleem looked towards me and said tartly, 'Maybe you should go and catch up with her. Tell her you and Ray'll sort something out. The way I see it, if Doug can get rid of her that easily and you're both too spineless to do anything about it, then he can also dispense with your services too, if and when the fancy takes him.'

'She's running.'

'Catch up with her. See that she's OK.'

'Maybe Ray should go?'

'Not me,' Ray said, 'I'm not nimble enough.'

Saleem smiled at Ray. 'Anyhow, me and Ray,' she said, 'need to have a quiet little chat.'

Ray's eyes bulged nervously at this prospect. I smiled to myself and slunk out.

Ten minutes later, after a cursory stroll around the sections of the park in which I was least likely to find Nancy – Christ, she would have been half way up Alderman's Hill by the time I'd left the house, and anyway, what could I have said to her if I did catch up with her? What could I promise? And how could I be sure that the words would come? I couldn't be sure – I found myself travelling past the main lake, past the ducks and clambering on to the bandstand and settling myself in a shady corner where I fully intended to dawdle for ten minutes before returning to the house, back to Ray and Saleem.

It was cool and green here, and the water sloshed to my left, and in the distance I could hear a spaniel barking as it ran for a ball, and the thwuck and the swish as it caught the ball and returned it. To my right, I could see one of the tennis courts, and one of the greenhouses, and I could also see, if I stretched my neck, a small man in a white shirt who was limbering up, bending and stretching and bending and stretching.

And I found a fuzzy rhythm in this corner. A wooziness. And as the lids on my eyes descended, cutting my view in half, I felt a terrible certainty, in my gut, in my soul, that nothing could change the way things were, it wasn't possible, because nature didn't work in jerks and starts, but in a rhythm, a cycle, a circle, and Doug, of all people, was aware of that fact. And so was I.

Then out of the blue, out of the sky, a fistful of sand landed in my face. I blinked, shook myself, and then a clod of soil landed to my left followed by a small geranium plant, then a further clod of soil.

I stood up and saw for the first time that the innocuous little man in the white shirt was bending and stretching in the middle of my newly planted flower bed, plum in the middle of my freshly planted flower bed, and he was yanking up plants and tossing them. My new geraniums, the spider plants, other things. This way and that. An arc of soil flew over him.

I jumped off the bandstand and made my way over to him. As I drew closer I saw that he was Chinese and wearing kung-fu robes and he was older than I'd initially thought – sixty or so – but his hair was black and his face was hooded, and something in it was scary, was withered, was fundamentally unpleasant.

And yet his expression was in such direct contrast to his body, his movements, which even in his present task were as fluid and beautiful as a seal's. I appraised his body as I approached, calculating my chances in the likelihood of any kind of physical confrontation.

He was small but he was also solid and thorough and focused; clenched like a little nugget, a meteorite. Plain like a stone. I drew closer to him, but he ignored me. I drew closer

26

still. I said, 'Excuse me. I think you'd better stop what you're doing.'

His head turned, a fraction. 'You fuck off.'

He wasn't nice. His voice was like a dry cork twisting in the neck of a bottle. A tight voice.

I said, again, 'I'd like you to stop what you're doing, immediately, please.'

He plucked a geranium, and weighed it in his hand, looked straight at me, took aim, and thwack! He hit me with it, in the centre of my chest. It had quite some clout, for a geranium. I stepped back slightly, and it was then that I thought I saw Doug, in the doorway of his greenhouse, and even from a distance it looked like Doug was smiling.

'You know him?'

Squeaking voice. I turned back. 'Pardon?'

He pointed towards Doug, 'You know him?'

'Who? Doug?'

'I have a message for him.'

'For Doug?'

'D'you know me?'

I glanced over towards Doug again, but Doug had disappeared, had gone. I guessed he'd withdrawn, back to his tomatoes.

'Do I know you? No. I don't know you.'

'I am Wu.' He offered me a small, slightly muddy hand. 'Shake.'

Gingerly, I offered him my hand. He took it and squeezed it and his grip was like steel.

'Wu! Wu!' he barked softly. 'Like a dog, huh?' And my hand was crumbling and grinding and liquidizing.

'Let go of my hand, please.'

Wu pulled me close to him, so close I could feel little sprays of his saliva on my neck as he spoke.

'Your friend,' he said, 'I don't like him and I don't want him near me. I don't want him watching me, see? All the time I feel his eyes on me. And you can tell him, from me, that a frog cannot turn into a green leaf.'

27

'I'll tell him. Let go of my hand.'

He lessened his grip a fraction, pulled me even closer, stood on his tip-toes and whispered directly into my ear, 'I hope I didn't break your knuckle.' Finally, after one more, gentle squeeze, he let go. He wiped his hands clean on his robes and walked off. Slowly, calmly, treading softly.

I looked down at my hand. I tried to wiggle my fingers. I could move my thumb but nothing else. My fingers were purple, the joints were white. The whole hand was burning. I ran over to the lake and dipped my fist in it. But the water didn't help to cool me. It was warm as saliva at its edges. I took my hand out, held it in front of me like a trophy, and went to find Doug.

Doug was watering some tomatoes in his greenhouse. The house was warm and had that rich smell of damp compost which always makes me feel like sneezing: a fine, ripe smell.

Doug watered his tomatoes with enormous tenderness. He didn't take his eyes off them as he spoke.

'So he got you, did he?'

I stood next to his marrows and his radishes, both of which seemed to be coming on well. The radishes were already the size of tennis balls. 'I think he broke my hand.'

'Wu. He's a devil.' Doug chuckled to himself before adding, 'I can't take my eyes of him. My fault he destroyed the bed. I can't stop myself from watching him and he's warned me. He gets irritable.' He chuckled again.

I said, 'I've never even seen him before.'

Doug moved on to the next bush.

'Phil, someone could squat down and shit on your foot and you'd hardly notice them.'

I let this pass. Pain had made me bold. My hand hurt so much that I could hardly contemplate any other kind of feeling. I said, 'I don't think you want to have too much to do with that man in the future, Doug.'

'Wu!' Doug said, delightedly. 'Did you see the way he moves around this place? Flowing, flowing. Like water. Like he owns the whole damn park. And the sky. That special kind of movement. Inside out. Round. That strange oriental kind of moving. Tip-toeing but very sure.'

'I think he broke my hand.'

Doug turned off the hose. 'I've been following him about since I moved into the house. Early in the morning he comes to the park, climbs over the fence before we even open, and he does all that strange, slow dancing. Tai Chi. I've been watching him, I even approached him for a talk but he didn't want disturbing. I think I broke his concentration,' Doug said, 'and so it's possible I've started getting on his nerves.'

'He said that. He told me to tell you that you were getting on his nerves. I don't think you should pester him any more.'

Doug gave this some thought and then for the first time he turned his eyes on me. 'That sudden violence,' he said cheerfully, 'I like it. I like the *idea* of it. It's clean.'

'He's destroyed the flower bed. I spent half the afternoon planting it.'

'He's cleaned it out,' Doug said, unperturbed. 'Good luck to him. I have plans for that section anyway,' he added, 'a couple of big ideas. Icing on the cake.'

'But for the time being . . .'

'And if I've learned one thing from that tough little man,' Doug said, 'it's that you've got to have your own vision and stick to it. Ignore the rest of life's radish.'

'Life's radish?' I echoed, bemused.

Doug nodded. 'No more rubbish. Only truth.'

He then moved a few feet across, fingered the bright shoot of a large onion and said, almost to himself, 'This one's going to be a giant. I can feel it. I can smell it.' He scratched his nose. 'Do you smell it, Phil?' He glanced over at me. 'Smell it, do you?'

'Smell what?'

Doug sucked his tongue, irritated. 'You don't see it, Phil, do you? You just don't see how there's a real logic to an onion. One layer inside another layer inside another layer. All circular. Like a maze. A puzzle. Nothing missing. No gaps. Just simple.'

My hand was swollen now. It had swelled up like a puffer fish. 'If he tries to assault me again,' I muttered, 'I'll call the police.'

Doug carried on talking to his onion, 'One layer inside another layer.'

'Doug. About Nancy . . .'

'Whosoever diggeth a pit, Phil, shall fall in it. Nancy dug her pit. She's fallen into it.'

'Even so . . .'

Doug began to scowl. 'I want big, Phil, and I want neat. Big, neat, clean, true. Not just the park itself, but everything. The whole lot. The business, the talking, the ideas. Big, *clean*, neat, true. None of that muddy stuff, none of that green fruit, nothing unripe, none of that murky water.'

I looked down at my hand.

'I'll fix the bed in the morning,' I said, 'before we open. I don't think I can replant right now with my fist all swollen.'

Doug waved me away with his hand, 'Go away, Phil. Go. I'm busy with this onion. There's work to do here.'

I hesitated.

'Phil,' Doug barked. 'Go away. Let's get tidy. And I don't just mean weeding and replanting. OK?'

I nodded. I retreated.

'Where's Ray?'

Saleem was in the kitchen alone. She had Cog on her lap and she was stroking him. Cog's purr almost lifted the tablecloth.

'He's gone,' she said, 'to the pub. You didn't find Nancy, I gather?'

'No.'

'Fuck. Your hand's all swollen. What did you do?'

'I crushed it in the mower.'

'You've been out mowing?'

'I was putting it away.'

'Is it broken?'

'No, the mower's fine.'

She knocked Cog off her lap. 'Let's see it.'

I backed off a fraction. 'It's in the barn. I locked it up for the night.'

She gazed at me, unsmiling. 'Do you seriously think I'm going to hurt you, Phil?'

'Hurt me? No.'

I inspected my shirt-front. Wu's geranium assault had left its mark.

'Sit down Phil. I want to talk to you.' Saleem pulled out a chair and pointed at it.

'Ray's expecting me. Maybe I'll go to casualty with this hand.'

'Sit. Screw Ray. Screw your hand.'

I sat down, but on the edge of the chair so she'd sense I wasn't staying.

'OK,' Saleem perched herself against the table. 'Picture the worst case scenario . . .'

I studied my hand. It was still smarting. I thought about the pain.

'If Doug gets any more erratic and irascible than he already is, then there's no way we can let him go to the meeting on Friday.'

'He has to go. No one else can.'

'You could.'

'Doug has to go. I can't go.'

'Why not?'

'I just can't. Doug needs our support. He needs to be kept on an even keel, that's all.'

'Ha!' Saleem rolled back on her hip, victorious. 'So even you've noticed that something's up. Even you, finally, have noticed.'

'I'm only saying . . .'

'Picture the worst case scenario.'

'It's hardly going to come to that.'

'If Doug can't go, you'll have no choice but to go yourself. Ray's a moron. You understand how the park works.'

31

'But I don't have anything to do with the business side of things. That's Doug's department.'

'You'd just have to acquaint yourself with a selection of the most salient facts, that's all. I could help you.' She pointed towards one of the kitchen drawers. 'It's all in there. The papers, the bills, receipts, accounts. Everything we need.'

'It won't come to that.'

'Look,' Saleem pushed herself up off the table, 'I've got something for you. It's kind of last-minute, but I think it might help.' She picked up her stick and disappeared from the kitchen.

Cog came and slithered around my ankles. My knuckles felt like they were growing. Expanding. I looked around and my eyes settled on a tea-cloth over by the sink. I stood up, grabbed hold of it, dampened it in some cold water and tried to apply it to my hand. Saleem returned.

'What're you doing?'

'I'm trying to tie this around my knuckles.'

Saleem was holding a book. She put it down on the table and came over. She snatched the tea-towel, wrung it out and tied it on firmly. I winced. Pain and her proximity left me squeamish.

'Sit.'

She pushed me down on to the chair again. She picked up the book. It had a red cover.

'See this?' She held the book up to me. It was called *I'm Not Angry, I'm Hurting* by Dr John Sledge. 'Guess what, Phil?'

'What?' I wished the book didn't have a red cover. Not red.

'You're not angry, Phil, you're hurting.'

I inspected my makeshift bandage. I said, 'I think I'm feeling a little of both, actually.'

Saleem ignored this.

'I went to a psychiatrist, after the accident,' she said, 'after the museum burned down and I lost my leg.' She paused for a moment and then grinned. 'Fuck all wrong with me, though. But for some reason, that quack gave me this book. Obviously, it's all bollocks. Most of it. But there's something in here, Phil, that I think might help us. Kind of like the inside of a nut.'

'A kernel.'

'Exactly.'

She paged through the book. She pushed the pages flat on Chapter four: 'How I Feel, How You Feel'. She handed me the book. 'Read.'

I closed the book. I said. 'I'll read it later. I think I should go and see Ray.'

'It's a quick fix,' Saleem said, undaunted, 'and if you're going to attend that meeting on Friday then we're going to need a quick fix, because you know and I know that you won't have the balls to stand up in front of five people and present a good case for our tender without some kind of divine intervention.'

'It won't come to that.'

'It might.'

She took the book back and opened it again. 'The main point Sledge makes is this, right. He says, it's not *what* happens in life that screws you up but how you *interpret* events. See? So sometimes, if you're very sensitive, then often it's not like bad things have actually happened, only that they feel bad to you. So it's all a question of getting things in proportion, yeah?'

I gave my sore knuckle a little squeeze so that the pain would distract me. A kind of anaesthetic.

'And right here's how you go about it. Chapter Four. Right here. Cognitive Behaviour Therapy. Something called the three Cs. Cool, calm, confident. Uh . . . rhythmic exercises and stuff. Breathing.'

I scratched my beard. 'Did Ray say he'd be in The Fox?'

Saleem looked up from the book. She suddenly wasn't as affable as she'd seemed before.

'You'd better listen to me, Phil. I'm not bullshitting you. I'm taking control of this situation and it's going to be a bumpy fucking ride.'

Her anger blew in my face like hot air from a hairdryer. Hot. Dry. She looked down at the book again. 'You've got to get stuff in proportion. You've got to do it quickly, that's all I'm saying. And it won't be easy.'

Cog jumped up on to the table next to her. He'd barely landed before she knocked him off with a vigorous swipe. He skidded as he landed on the tiles.

'You and I are going out together, right now, and we are going up on to the High Street, to the chemist's, and you are going to walk in there, straight to the counter, and in a clear, loud voice you are going to ask the assistant for a packet of extra-small condoms.'

I shook my head. I continued staring down at the tiles.

'OK, so it sounds stupid, but there's a reason behind it . . .'

'I'm not doing that.'

'It's therapeutic. Kind of like embarrassing yourself on purpose. Taking it to the limit. Forcing yourself. Taking control of embarrassing situations and so taking the sting out of them.'

Sting. Saleem. Cog stood by the kitchen door. I wanted to be where Cog was. I wanted to be Cog. I shook my head. Outside I could hear something. Footsteps, a door opening, a metallic jangle. The engine of Nancy's truck bursting into life.

Nancy. I looked up and over towards the window. Saleem was staring at me. I didn't meet her eye. And then I heard her voice whispering under the growl of the truck. Lower than the truck and growlier. She said, 'And you care about this place, and you care about Nancy, but you don't have the guts to do anything. You won't speak up. You won't even do that. That one small thing. And I'd give up my fucking body, and Doug'd give up his fucking soul. But you, you won't give anything.'

Saleem threw the book down onto my lap, picked up her stick, left me. I heard the front door slam. Outside I heard female voices. And whispering.

RAY WAS ON HIS third pint by the time I'd arrived at The Fox. He was perched on a stool by the bar. The pub wasn't too full, although Ray's enough of a man to fill any room. His arms are giant leeks, white leeks tipped with two artichoke paws, a full fist of fingers which he wiggles and he waggles to great dramatic effect.

I pulled up a stool for myself. Ray inspected my hand.

'Did Nancy do that?'

'No.'

'Saleem?'

'Let me just say something, Ray.'

He looked up, surprised by my determined tone. 'What?'

I thought for a moment. 'I just think we've got to make a real effort to keep Doug calm. Especially over the next couple of days.'

'OK.'

I smiled. It was so easy with Ray. And I said, 'I don't think we should involve Saleem too much in the park's affairs either.'

Ray suddenly looked uneasy, he fidgeted on his stool. 'Saleem's quite involved,' he said, 'already.'

'Well she doesn't need to be any more involved, that's all I'm saying.'

'No,' Ray took a sip of his beer.

'Doug's doing fine.'

Ray took another sip. He smacked his lips. 'You're right,' he said. He ordered me a pint, paid, passed it over. As he passed it I said, almost casually, almost incidentally, 'And the China-man . . .'

'Wu.'

'You know about him?'

Ray knew. He knew. Ray, it turned out, knew more than I'd thought. Ray, it turned out, had served as a confidant, a gatherer of scraps, an unobservant observer.

People feel they can trust Ray. They trust his gormlessness, his softness, his delicious, harmless squelchiness.

35

People mention things to Ray and they know that no judgement will be forthcoming, no private reckoning will take place in the cavern of Ray's brain, no stern moral hypothesis will be formulated and delivered. Ray is a sponge. Ray is natural, is, above all other things (and how could it be otherwise, really?), *himself*.

Something dawned on me. A kind of shame. No one tells me stuff. No one tells me anything. Not of their own accord. My head is so full of other things, of myself, of itself, that no one ever bothers telling me anything else.

'No one told me this stuff, Ray,' I said at one point, during a conversational hiatus. 'No one mentioned any of this to me.'

'You're lucky,' Ray answered blithely. 'You've got your own business going on. You've got,' he paused for greater emphasis, 'you've got a *secret life*, up there,' he tapped his skull.

'And you don't?'

He grinned, 'I've got all the outside stuff. That's plenty.'

By Ray's fourth pint I wasn't worried any more, not shy to be spoken to, not conscious of his gaze. Ray's eyes were watery, wandering; tadpoles in the jelly of his face. 'You want to know about Wu?' he asked. 'Well, if you want to know about Wu, then first you have to know about Doug and Mercy and the Anniversary Dinner.'

'I do?'

He nodded. 'You see, I don't understand all this business myself. It's only that Saleem said something and then Doug mentioned something else. It's not like anything fits together in any way. Nothing like that. But I keep picking up this information and slotting it away . . .'

'But Wu . . . ?'

'Remember three weeks ago? Before Doug moved in with Saleem? Before all this weird stuff? Doug and Mercy's thirtieth wedding anniversary. That's where it started . . .'

'Mercy and the diarrhoea, Saleem said something . . .'

Ray nodded. 'That's the one. Just listen,' he said. 'You won't hardly believe it.'

And slowly, slowly, with commendable precision, Ray rolled open his canvas and covered it with colour. And each stroke was perfect, each touch, each piece of his narrative fitted, each portion, each serving, so neat and geometrical, *every* element, a balance. Like he was neatly laying squares of turf down for a brand new lawn.

'Picture it,' Ray said, his eyes sparkling, 'Friday night, three weeks ago. Italian restaurant. La Bruschetta on Green Lanes. Doug's all dressed up for dinner. Jacket, tie. Mercy's wearing a new dress. Doug's been busy all day working on the accounts for the park. Things are tight. The budget's stretching thin . . . yeah, well, who cares, because they're out for a special night together. Thirty years! That's something worth celebrating.

'Now here's the important part, right, pay attention. Doug is perfectly happy. Four words: *Doug is perfectly happy!* He's got other things on his mind, naturally, other pressures: work, the park, money, their gas boiler might be on the blink . . . yeah, well, but everything's fine, and the waiter comes over to their table and they order their starters.

'Mercy has Parma ham. Great. Doug's about to have the same – he always follows Mercy's lead in culinary matters, that's just the way it is between them – and then his eye swerves, he looks down the menu, and his gaze settles on the words "prawn cocktail". He thinks: what the hell. I'm thirty years married. Time for something new. Prawn cocktail.

'Doug looks up at the waiter and he says "Prawn cocktail, please." And Mercy stares at him with a strange expression on her face. He stares back at her. "What's up?" he says. "Doug, what made you choose that prawn cocktail?" He gives it some thought. He says, "Do I need a reason?" She shrugs.

'They order the rest of their meal, their drinks, and off the waiter goes. Fine. Except Doug can't help noticing that Mercy's expression is a little bit brighter, a little bit tighter.

'The starters arrive. Doug digs in. Mercy's staring at his prawns. She's not touched her ham yet. She says, "Doug, why did you order that prawn cocktail when you know we never have prawns?" Doug puts down his fork. He says, "Now what? What's the big problem with the prawns?" Mercy says, "Remember our very first date?" Doug gives it some thought. He remembers. Mercy says, "Well, on that occasion I had prawns." Doug is flummoxed. So what? And he turns his mind back to that very first date.

'And the truth is – and he remembers it – that he didn't much like Mercy when he first met her. Not for any particular reason, but there was no spark between them, not on his side, at least, and he firmly believes in a spark. He's romantic like that, although you'd be hard pressed to imagine it now.

'Anyway, he remembers their first date, thirty years ago. Remembers it clearly, how, at the beginning, on their way to the restaurant, things were really dragging, and he was wondering why he agreed to go, and he was thinking about how his parents knew Mercy's parents and how Mercy's brother was at the same cricket club, all this stuff.

'And then Doug remembers, with a smile, how it happened, during the meal, how something peculiar, something completely unexpected happened. They were on their second course, they'd been talking, and suddenly, out of the blue, he saw that Mercy was brighter than he'd thought, and sparky, and nervous, and she had this restlessness, this vivacity. And the candle on the table flickered its light on her and she was beautiful. Beautiful.

'In that instant, Doug knew that there was a spark. Right there, in his heart. And she wasn't pushy, she wasn't slow, she wasn't any of the things he'd thought she was. She was fine, jumpy, mysterious; a thoroughbred.

'Doug remembered. *Thirty years!* He grinned to himself. He picked up his spoon. Mercy was glaring. He put down his spoon. Now what? What's the problem? "I hate prawns, Doug," Mercy mutters. "That very first date we went on, I had prawns as a starter and they nearly ruined everything."

'Well you can imagine, Doug is staring at her like she's crazy. "I mean it, Doug," she says. "I had some prawns and they gave me the quickest and the worst and the strongest dose of food poisoning I've ever had. How I sat through that meal I'll never know. My stomach was a volcano, my head was on fire. I could barely hold my fork."

'Bang! Suddenly Doug's mind is clicking and whirring, turning over and everything's playing back in slow motion. And he realizes, it dawns on him, it strikes him that Mercy is not the woman he thought she was. She wasn't the woman he fell in love with. He fell in love with – and this is the best part or the worst part according to how you look at it – he fell in love with a small dose of *staphi cocci*. That's bacteria, incidentally.

'You see, Mercy wasn't that vivacious woman, that flighty, peachy, jumpy thoroughbred. She was a boring person with a gastric disorder. But Doug hadn't seen it. He'd duped himself. He'd sold himself down the river. Bang! Just like that. Doug had built his house on sand. Doug had been living a lie. It was over. That was it. He moved out of their home that very same night.'

Ray rested his head on the bar, sideways, and stared at me. I was gawping.

'Ray,' I said, 'I've never heard such a pile of absolute garbage.'

Ray was unfazed. 'Later I saw Mercy,' he said, 'and she was sobbing her eyes out because Doug had told her she was never the person he thought she was. She just didn't get it, and I didn't get it either. I told her so. I said, "He's having a brainstorm. Men sometimes go funny at fifty." She said, "Women go funny too but they don't make such a song and dance about it." I said, "Fair enough." That's all I could say.'

'Is there anything else?'

Ray sighed. 'Well, Saleem thinks the problem is longer term. The big vegetables in the greenhouse. His obsession with getting the bandstand built. Wu. She thinks Doug's having all these weird thoughts about religion and truth and culture and the Mercy thing's just a part of it. She says she hears him talking to himself at night, having whole conversations all on his own. She says Doug's been muttering stuff to her about how events all go in a circle and that everything inside has to come outside and that all actions should be true actions and direct actions. He's private and secretive but also evangelical. You'd think it'd be hard to be all these things at once but Doug seems to manage it.

'Anyhow, Saleem says that if he talks to anyone for a period longer than five minutes then it becomes extremely apparent that he's very disturbed indeed. Very disturbed. She said he can't go to the meeting on Friday because it'll be as plain as her face that he's as mad as a hatter. We'll lose the tender.'

'Forget about Saleem, Ray,' I said, 'Doug might be thinking a lot of strange things but it hasn't affected us directly yet. I'm sure we can sort out the business with Nancy during the two weeks she's working out her notice. He'll come around. And there's no reason for us to believe that the meeting won't be just fine. It's all a question of keeping things in proportion.

'And if what Doug says is true, and things do move in a circle, then maybe Doug will get back to how he used to be eventually. Maybe even quite soon if everything stays calm.'

Ray sighed again, even deeper this time. 'It's true, then,' he determined, out of nowhere, 'what Saleem said about you being a man of integrity.'

'What?'

Ray sighed again. 'I might have some crisps,' he muttered, and then, 'Maybe you're right. Maybe we should just bide our time and keep things in proportion. And maybe Doug's right too, about the circle and everything coming back to where it started. You never know. You can't tell with life, can you? What's around the next corner?'

Ray finished his drink with a flourish and ordered three packets of smoky bacon.

I TESTED OUT the physical viability of my damaged hand during my walk home from the pub. First off, I tried bending the fingers with the aid of my undamaged hand, then I tried bending them without assistance, next I tried to form them into a kind of half-fist, and finally I pulled out Dr John Sledge's *I'm Not Angry, I'm Hurting* from my jacket pocket and tested whether I could fold my fingers round it and bear its weight. After performing this final task with some ease I decided that maybe things weren't as bad in dextral terms as they'd initially seemed.

Home is the ground floor of a nice house on Broomfield Road which has been converted into two self-contained flats. The road runs adjacent to the park on its southern perimeter. The flat used to belong to my grandmother and now it belongs to me. Consequently, it has a dusty old chintz and velvet feel to it, but is spartan too, like the home of someone in two minds about the nature and possibilities of interior decor. And although by instinct I'm a small, shy, dozy creature, happy holed up, solitary, contained, in fact I get claustrophobic inside and prefer a place where there is no roof, only sky, and a high sky at that.

I held Dr John Sledge in my hand and I swung my arm. I sniffed the tea-towel, which was still damp, but drier now, and musty, robust, sassy with the tang of sweat. Using my good hand, I felt inside my pocket for my keys. And then I saw her. On my doorstep.

Saleem was glaring. 'Where the hell have you been? I've been round here twice. I've been waiting for absolutely bloody hours.'

Saleem, incongruously, on my doormat. Was she a figment? A fragment? An ugly spectre? An invasive sylph? A sprite?

I tested out my voice. It was steady. 'What are you doing here?'

She carried right on scowling. 'We've got to talk. Now.'

I was tired, suddenly, 'Can't it wait? Would you mind?'

She shook her head. 'It can't wait. Open the door. Let me inside. I'm freezing.'

It was a warm night. I didn't want to open the door. If I let her in she might never leave, might take up residence, squat, like she did in the park keeper's house. She had that adhesive, that sticky quality which wouldn't come out in the wash.

'You're pissed,' she muttered, watching as I fumbled with my keys.

'I had three pints and I'm perfectly sober.'

'Great in a fucking crisis. First thing you do is reach for the bottle.'

I took my keys out. 'There's no crisis and I'm not drunk.'

'Let me smell your breath.' Uninvited, unexpected, she pushed her face into mine, sniffed, grinned and then took this opportunity to bite me, sharply, impishly on the nose.

'Oh Christ.' Why did she do that? Her tongue was a cattle prod. She was a ball of venom, slobbering on me.

She cackled. 'Open up. Make me wait out here any longer and I'll fuck you up the arse with my stump. And remember,' she added, 'I've been standing all the while on only one sure limb, which is twice as tiring.' She knocked my shins with her stick.

She has that capacity to offend, Saleem, to hurt, mortally. I hate that in her. I'd like to hurt her back but I just don't have it in me. I'd like to injure her, knock the other leg out from under her, just once.

I opened the door. She pushed past me and bounded into the kitchen, pulled wide the oven door and switched the gas on full.

'What're you doing?'

'Gassing myself. What d'you think? I'm cold. Give me a match.'

'If you want to light it then use the ignition.'

'I want a match. I'm cold. Give me a bloody match right now or else.'

She was cold-blooded. An amber mamba. I gave her the match and said, 'Switch it off first. Don't just . . .'

Floooom! A gust of blue flame bellowed out of the oven. Saleem didn't move or shirk. 'Yeah! I love that.'

She stared at the flame for a while, grinning, while it filled her irises and made them yellower. Then she snatched her eyes away, blinked, pulled out a chair and sat down.

'OK,' she said, 'So you don't know why I'm here, do you? Maybe you think I've come to appraise your living quarters. I've never even been in your house before. You never invited me.' She looked around the kitchen. 'Yeah, not bad. If things go wrong at the park after Friday I could easily make a den for myself here. Wouldn't take too much adjusting.'

She smiled, apparently well satisfied with this pronouncement, waiting, now, for a response.

I didn't respond. I said, 'What's the problem?'

'Make me a cuppa.'

'It's late.'

'Go on, I'm freezing.'

'It's nearly midnight. I want to go to bed, if you don't mind.'

'Make me a cuppa and then I'll come with you.'

'I haven't got any milk.'

'Fine.' She stood up, picked up her stick from the table. 'Let's fuck.'

My temples throbbed. I took one deep breath and then another. 'Why are you here Saleem?'

She grinned at me, dug her hand into the pocket of the large denim jacket she was wearing and pulled out a sheet of paper.

'See this?' She passed it to me. I took it with my good hand. 'Nancy left it out for Doug on the kitchen table. It's from the nursery in Southend she visited today.'

'So?'

'Well read it, stupid.'

I inspected it.

'Look at it,' she said, excitedly. 'Privet!'

She nudged me between my ribs with her elbow.

'Privet!' she exclaimed, yet again. 'And all the while I'd been

43

thinking *private*. Doug's been going on about being *private*, but I'd got it all wrong, see? He meant privet.'

Saleem had lost it.

'No I don't see.'

I did see, however, that Doug had ordered literally a ton of the stuff. He'd spent a fortune on it. Three hundred pounds which I was certain the park didn't possess.

Saleem eyed me inquisitively. 'And there I was,' she said, 'thinking that the park was broke and that you could all barely afford to put petrol in the mower.'

'It's nothing,' I said, calmly. 'I already had an inkling about this.' My words sounded half-formed.

Saleem snorted, 'Phil, you're so bloody transparent. Like a square of polythene.'

I folded up the receipt and handed it back to her.

'Privet, private,' she continued, speculatively, 'one letter different.'

'I can't dispute that.'

She pushed her skinny face up close to mine, 'Doug's going to do something very stupid, and he's going to do it soon, and it's going to screw everything up.'

If I'd stepped back at this point I'd have ended up in the oven. Warm air against the back of my legs was already making me prickle.

'And where would you be without the park, huh? And where would I be? If someone new takes over the tender they'd be bound to evict me. They wouldn't care about my *history* with the place. Not strangers.'

'It won't come to that.'

She drew even closer, 'It might. It just might.'

And I felt something strange, in my midriff. Saleem's finger. It had threaded its way through a gap in my shirt, between the buttons, and was poking, sharply, pointedly, into my navel. Then it rotated, like I was a clockwork mouse and she was winding me up.

'I must just quickly tell you,' she whispered, 'the way I see it. It's like this, right: we've all been surfing, on the water's surface, on top of a wave, sure-footed, and time has passed fairly comfortably, but now, all of a sudden, we've fallen off our boards and into the ocean. We're swallowing water, it's icy cold, it's wet, it's salty, and when we come up for air, it feels different. Very different. Not like the air we were surfing in before. Better. And every breath, every breath . . .'

I pushed her away. 'Stop that.'

She stared at her finger for a moment, sniffed it, and then placed it in her mouth, sucked it, winked, removed it and said loudly, 'Grab this opportunity and make the most of it.'

'What opportunity?'

'OK, so fine,' she was suddenly businesslike, 'I said this afternoon that I was the one to change things. But now . . .' She shrugged. 'I'm entrusting all this shit to you, handing it all over. For the time being.' She grabbed my arm. 'Wanna take me now or wait till morning?

'Handing what over?'

'You look knackered,' she added, letting go of my arm, her top lip curling. 'Better wait.'

She grabbed her stick and bounded out.

Thursday

SLEEP CAME AND WENT like a slug crawling over my belly. I woke at five and lay in bed, still half-dressed. I had two unusual bed-mates. Firstly, the tea-towel, which had loosened itself from my wrist and had journeyed up my arm until it found a niche around my shoulder, under my armpit.

Secondly, incongruously, Dr John Sledge's book, which was lying on the pillow next to my head. I appraised its redness. I prodded it with my nose. I put out a hand, gingerly, picked it up, opened its pages and blinked at it. *You can't see the world through anyone else's eyes*, Dr Sledge said, *only your own. There's nothing wrong with being who you are. But let's try to make sure that you like who you are. Let's be sure that you like yourself. Because if you don't like yourself, how do you expect anyone else to like you? And if you don't know yourself, how can you expect anyone else to want to know you?*

I looked to the top of the page. It said, Chapter Two: 'Knowing Yourself'. I closed the book and inspected my bad hand. It was bruised, had the dominant colours of a fine Red Oak Leaf lettuce. Purple and red and a darkish blue. Green on its edges and a slurried yellow.

I lay back and tried to think about things. I had a lot to digest. But sometimes digesting isn't as easy, as natural a process as it might be. You see, I have the kind of brain that doesn't link things too well. Admittedly, I was the recipient of a whole, big, scruffy bundle of information, but most of it was words and feelings and hearsay, and these things mean little to me, mean nothing to me until I can see the proof of them with my own two eyes.

A wholesaler might answer in the affirmative when I ask whether the hollyhock seedlings I've just purchased are all a single colour, but when they grow, when they flower, only then can I be truly sure. And it's not suspicion or cynicism that makes me this way. I'm just stupid and dumb like a dozy mongrel. I do things and I do things and I believe things when I see them with my own eyes. That's when. Only then.

49

I've got some camomile tea that I made myself, that I grew myself, that I drink at night sometimes or to relax me. I got up and drank a cup. It tasted like a bundle of hay. I pulled on my shoes and I walked outside, still feeling like I had a whole farmyard on my tongue.

It was early. I was earlier than usual. I wanted to check up on a couple of things, iron out hitches, smooth stuff over. I wanted to make sure that nothing bad could happen, to try to keep Doug padded up for the day in a soft swab of cotton wool. It felt necessary.

The park wasn't open yet. I unlocked one of the gates with my key and went in. It was getting light, like the sky was slowly growing accustomed to having the sun spill out all its pale guts on to it. No clouds, only a roof in the heavens the grey-white colour of spittle.

It was so quiet, and the quiet was like a kiss. Soft and gentle, and all the plants were waking up in the sure caress of this silence, yawning and stretching and swallowing the dew. Even here, even in the city, this little green heart was pumping and throbbing and murmuring.

I followed the path to the barn. I paused for a second, stared over at Nancy's truck which was parked where it had been the previous afternoon. Everything was still. I went into the barn and pulled out some tools: a fork, a hoe, a small trowel, and headed off in the direction of the damaged flower bed. But I reached something else before I reached the bed, someone else. Wu. In a corner, filling the path between a rhododendron and the herb garden.

Wu. Dancing, just like I'd been told. In his loose robes, with his leg in the air, moving slowly up and around, he looked like a gannet, a heron, the topmost trumpet of a white lily, touched by the wind and bending its neck, swooning.

I stopped in my tracks. My hand gave a little twitch, like it remembered, like its damaged flesh had a memory. Wu hadn't seen me, or at least gave no indication of having seen me but continued with his tiny movements, began painting slow, splendid letters in the air with his hands, packed the air with his palms, shifted it, organized it. Air, only air.

I turned back on myself, slipped through the rockery, past the lake, over and around, and ended up, after this small diversion, where I wanted to be. Facing my ruined bed, my back to Doug's greenhouse.

What was it that made me turn? The sound of a door hinge squeaking? Something metallic which wasn't the close, clinking sound of the tools I was holding? Nothing like that. A little message. An inkling.

And I did turn. What made me turn? And I saw that the door was ajar. The greenhouse door. This was the first sign. The door was ajar. It made me shudder, the idea of the door being left open, the warm air escaping. I dropped my tools and walked over. I could smell something. Rich soil, compost. Sap.

I pulled the door wide and walked in, checking the temperature gauge to my left, immediately, out of instinct. Cog whisked around my ankles and made me shudder again.

I looked around me. It was terrible. Everything was up and out and overturned. Mud and dirt and water. Wretched vegetables – those giant things, those protein-pumped, overlarge, swollen creatures – scratched and hacked and bruised and bleeding, tossed and chopped and kicked around. On the floor. Corpses, partially buried. Ruined. A massacre.

My mind worked in its own natural way. I didn't think of vandals, only of Doug, that someone hated Doug very badly or that Doug hated himself very badly. A stupid group of thoughts, like my mind was a collection of dried flowers, ornate and complex, but not as good as the real thing, the fresh thing, not at all.

I moved from the greenhouse and went outside again, closing the door behind me, securing it. What did this *mean*? How could I know what it meant until I could see what it meant with my own two eyes? And in the distance, beyond the herb garden, behind the rhododendron, I saw the slightest, whitest, spitefullest little figure. I saw him.

When did I pick up the hoe? I don't remember. Only Wu. I saw him and I wondered idly, was he mad or was he only different? Was he mad or only different? Then I was next to him. I saw him. Wu. Wu's eyes, full of the sky. I saw his eyes. I saw myself in them. And I thought . . . so all this had been going on? This mess, this madman, Doug and everything? All this had been going on even while everything else carried on too, the spring, the summer, the showers, the flowers?

Suddenly Nancy was next to me. 'Phil.'

'What have you done?'

I couldn't see Nancy, I was looking at Wu, I was speaking to Wu. I glared at him. He didn't seem in the least bit concerned. Very slowly, very slowly, he brought his arms and his legs down from the sky and into a kind of repose.

'Huh?'

'Do you know what you've done? Do you know?'

Wu seemed nonplussed. 'You want me to answer your questions? Huh? Yes. No. Yes. No. Huh?'

I was holding the hoe, horizontally. I gripped it. I didn't even stop to wonder what Nancy was doing. Why she was here.

Wu took several, small steps towards me and then stopped. He then took another small step forward. I braced myself.

'Give me that,' he said, pointing at the hoe.

'Give it to me, Phil,' Nancy said, because she was there, right next to me, and she took hold of the hoe and pulled it from me. But Wu was still moving, like I still had the hoe and he had every intention of taking it away from me. Slowly, he pushed the flat of his palm forwards, towards me, as though nudging a book or a drink or a flower in my direction. Closer and closer. I watched it, dazed, dazzled, and then it touched me. This slow hand hit me like a hammer in my chest. Until . . . yes! I was flying through the air, like a pancake or an omelette, twirling – a stingray – whirling and twisting. Up and up.

What a revelation! It wasn't at all dramatic. Not in the least how it should have been. His hand had been soft and then stronger than anything. And now I was flying, and I had time to think about all kinds of stuff, to notice that the holly still needed pruning, to remember how muddy Nancy's hands had been, to see that in the centre of the rockery there was clover. And it was flowering purply. It was far and then it was close and my nose was in it.

A while after I landed I felt a jolt. My arm was twisted, slung under me. I was winded. I felt, just a little, like sleeping.

OH, THIS WAS NICE. Kind of wet and slippery and I was moving without any effort. But, thinking about it, something was hurting, was hurting. A bump and a rucking and a grazing. A long distance away I heard a voice, a tight little voice, unfamiliar, which was saying, 'Can't force flow. Flow flows.' Flow *flows*.

Actually, the more I thought about it – and, be assured, there was no rush, no reason to rush – the more I gave it thought, the less happy I felt. My head was banging on the ground. My arm was aching, turned under me. I was being dragged. I felt mud and grass and then I felt gravel. My beard was so full of it. Bits of stone finding a home. Until, finally, I was still.

Something happened then, but I was no part of it. The gravel shifted, right up close to me, and then my face was wrapped in a warm, soft towel and a vapour darkened everything.

'Hello Phil. Hello Phil. Hello.'

'Wah?'

Shit. That was me.

I opened my eyes. Saleem had her face up close to mine and she was covered in blood – her cheek and her hand.

'Don't be shocked. I'm not hurt. This is your blood.'

'Oh.'

She wiped at her face with a piece of tissue while she said, 'Nancy's here. She dragged you in.'

Nancy materialized in front of me. 'I dragged you in. I'm really sorry. I'd never have taken the hoe away if I thought he was going to attack you. He's so powerful for a little fella. Like David Carradine in *Kung Fu*.'

'Where's Doug?'

Saleem had a bowl full of warm water and a roll of kitchen towel.

'He's upstairs. Still in bed.'

She leaned over me again and applied something damp to my cheek. 'Want to know what kind of injuries you sustained?'

'Uh, I feel OK.'

'Well, apart from the odd cut and graze, I think you broke your nose and sprained your arm. Maybe you sprained your ankle too. It's swelling out a bit.'

My ribs hurt when I inhaled. I tried to sit up, still woozy. 'What time is it?'

Nancy checked her watch, and I noticed again how dirty her hands were. Muddy hands.

'About half-seven.'

My arm did feel bad. We were in the kitchen. I was on the floor.

'I think · might like to sit on a chair.'

Nancy helped me up.

'Should we call the police?' she asked, settling me down again with a small huff of exertion.

'We can't call the police,' Saleem said quickly. 'We'd be fucking ourselves over.'

I was mystified by this response. 'Doug will probably want us to call them,' I said. 'That Chinese devil destroyed Doug's greenhouse before he assaulted me.'

Saleem expressed no surprise at this. Nancy didn't either. 'In that case,' Saleem said, 'we should really let Doug decide whether he wants to get the police involved or not. They're his vegetables, after all. And you . . .' She stared at me for a moment with an almost fond indifference. 'You'll mend.'

After a short pause she turned to Nancy and said pointedly, 'Aren't you in a hurry to unload that privet or something?'

Nancy shuffled her feet. 'I suppose so. I was just worried about Phil . . .'

'Actually,' Saleem said, 'I think we should tell Phil about where you're supposed to be going today.' Saleem turned towards me again. 'Guess where Nancy's going?'

'I don't know.'

'Tell him, Nancy.'

Nancy walked over to the sink and washed her hands. She spoke with her back to me, over her shoulder. 'Doug's got me going to Southend again for some more privet.'

'Privet? How much more?'

'Loads. And on Friday, too.'

'Did he give you any order forms?'

'Yeah.'

'Can I have a quick look at them?'

'I'll get them later. They're in the truck.'

Saleem butted in, 'D'you think you might be concussed?' she asked, purely, it seemed, out of interest, as though she and Nancy had had a small wager on this possibility. I was about to answer and then I heard a movement upstairs, a creaking.

'Doug's up,' I said, panicking, 'What shall we do? Maybe I could get to the greenhouse and tidy things up a bit if you two could try and keep him here for a while.'

I tried to stand up. I nearly managed it, but something buckled. 'I've got to start unloading,' Nancy said, sounding blank somehow, avoiding my eyes. She went out. I gazed after her, confounded.

'You can't hide things from Doug, Phil,' Saleem said calmly. 'He smells trouble at fifty paces.'

Doug was on the landing now. I could hear him. Then he was on the stairs, descending.

'Also,' Saleem added, 'I didn't want to say anything before, but in case you were determined to call the police, I'm not entirely sure that it was Wu who destroyed the greenhouse.'

'What?'

Doug was behind the door, right behind it. He was at the door. He was pressing some of his weight on to the door handle. I saw the handle move, down, up again, saw the door push inwards, towards me, and behind it . . . Doug. *Doug.* Square-chinned, resolute, hinged. Hanging on, like the door, but only just. I watched as Doug took his hand from the handle and I watched as the door closed behind him, smoothly, quietly, automatically.

Doug stood there and appraised me. He drank me in, slowly, and then he said, 'Phil, there's something hanging out of your nose. Looks like a big, raw, red caterpillar.'

He went and switched on the kettle. Saleem said, 'There's tea already in the pot.'

Doug grunted appreciatively, switched the kettle off again and took himself a mug off the mug-tree. 'I'm only telling you,' Doug added, lifting an eyebrow in my direction, 'because I'd find it difficult to eat breakfast with that thing just hanging there out of your nostril.'

Saleem handed me a piece of kitchen towel. I did the best I could. I pulled at the clot, manually at first, and the jelly came out and kept on coming like I was unravelling a dark, dense, red jelly brain through my nostril. When the jelly finally dissolved into loose blood, I blew my nose vigorously, rolled what I'd gathered into the tissue, pinched the bridge of my nose and stared up at the ceiling.

Doug was pouring himself some tea. Saleem – who was staring at me with a kind of fascinated disgust, hypnotised by the mighty clot – tore her eyes away when it had finished coming and said, 'Doug, Phil was just saying how someone broke into your greenhouse and totally wrecked everything.'

My mouth fell open. I think I stopped breathing, for a second. Doug stopped pouring.

'What did you say?'

I continued staring at the ceiling. 'Doug,' I said, 'I'm sure the damage isn't terminal. Some of the plants will be fine. It was only stupid vandals.'

Doug said nothing. He put down the teapot and walked out. I heard him slipping on his shoes in the hallway, and then I heard the front door slamming. I tried to stand up.

Saleem walked over to the sink. 'Doug's not going to be wanting his tea now,' she said, cheerfully. 'Do you want it?'

I was hot on Doug's heels, well, warm on his heels because I wasn't finding it too easy to walk. My ankle kept rolling, like

I was strolling on a ship in a high wind, up on deck, trying to keep my balance.

Outside, Nancy was standing by the rear flap of her truck, staring off into the distance, after Doug – his retreating back. She was cradling a small privet plant in her arms. As I staggered past her I said, 'Nancy, whatever you do, don't go to Southend for any more privet until I've had a word with Ray first.'

She put the tree down and trailed for a few paces behind me.

'Phil, how did he take it?'

'What?'

'Doug. What did he say?'

'He didn't say anything. Not yet, anyway.'

'He'll be all right, though?'

'This is probably the very worst thing that could've happened.'

'The very worst thing,' she parroted, speculatively, and then shouted, 'Hang on,' and sprinted off in the direction of the house. I carried on walking. After thirty seconds she was back again. She caught up with me just before the first lake.

'Here,' she panted, passing me one of Saleem's walking sticks. Saleem kept a small umbrella stand full of them just inside the front door.

Nancy handed me a stick which had a handle carved into a hare's head. It was a beautiful thing.

'Don't put too much weight on your bad leg, you'll only make it worse.'

I took the stick.

'I'm sorry,' she added, sounding it, 'about you getting hurt and Doug getting hurt.'

'It's nobody's fault.'

I twisted my hand around the hare's head.

'And don't put too much weight on your bad arm, either.'

'Thanks.' I took a few experimental steps forward. Nancy didn't walk with me. She hung back, remaining stationary.

I walked on. It was easier with the stick, but still slow. And in all honesty, I was glad of the time it took me to get to the greenhouse. I was almost glad of the pain. It was a kind of empathy. If not with Doug – he was a complex creature and I was obliged to find my own level, emotionally – then at least with his spoiled and battered vegetables.

'I'm sure the damage isn't terminal.'

Doug looked up and over, towards me. 'I think you said that earlier,' he muttered, witheringly. He was standing in the centre of the debris, inhaling the chaos.

'This shouldn't have happened,' he said, finally, 'It's all *wrong*.'

'You know, it might be possible to replant a couple of the tomatoes. Some of the radishes look all right too.'

'The tomatoes?'

Doug bent down and picked up one of the tomatoes which had detached itself from its plant. He held it in his hand like it was a cricket ball, a large cricket ball.

'You'd better get out of here,' he said, dispassionately, 'before I lose my temper.'

I was deciding whether to take his advice and leave when Doug clenched the tomato he was holding in his fist, took a couple of quick steps to build up momentum and then hurled it at me. I ducked. It flew past me, just to my left and struck glass, the pane closest to the door, striking it, splitting, shattering the glass.

Doug bent over and picked up an onion. He weighed it in his hand. 'D'you know what the worst part is?' Doug asked, still sounding as calm as anything.

I felt something warm on my top lip.

'You're bleeding,' Doug said. 'I don't want blood all over the floor in here.'

I mopped at my nose with my sleeve. The sight of blood seemed to pacify Doug again, even if he wasn't actually directly responsible for it.

'The worst part is that I must've left the door unlocked. But I know in my gut that I would never have done that. In my *gut*.'

Doug dropped the onion and walked over to the door. 'See that? No sign of a forced entry. Nothing broken.'

'Maybe they picked the lock.'

Doug bent down and stared at the lock intently, as though waiting for it to tell him something. Eventually he straightened up again and said, 'I don't think so.'

He turned his back to the door and appraised the devastation before him. 'I could swear to you that I locked that door,' he said, 'but I *can't* have. D'you know what that means, Phil? How it feels?'

I shook my head.

'It feels like I can't trust my own instincts on this one. I can't trust my own instincts. And if I can't trust my instincts, what can I trust? Who can I trust? Nothing. Nobody.'

Doug spent a moment considering his words. They seemed to please him. He crossed his arms. My nose was still bleeding.

'Red blood,' Doug said, 'Red, red, red blood.' He cleared his throat. 'There's only one way to get around this.'

I looked up, hoping Doug was about to respond rationally, *hoping*. Unfortunately his eyes were dark and clear. He uncrossed his arms. 'My instincts tell me this,' he said, 'and I shouldn't trust them because they've already lead me astray . . .' He inhaled deeply. 'You can only match this kind of gesture,' he indicated towards the mess and the mud with a grand sweep of his arm, 'you clan only match this kind of gesture with an even *bigger* gesture of your own.'

I weighed up this notion in my mind. An even bigger gesture. I didn't really get it but I knew it wouldn't necessarily be a good thing. I said, 'We could call that kind of response an escalation, Doug, and I don't know if things that go up, things that get bigger, are always . . . uh . . . good.'

Doug appreciated my insight but would have none of it. 'Nope,' he said, determinedly, 'getting bigger. That's the natural order of things . . . Clarity,' he added, 'cleanness. Big and neat. That's what I'm after.'

My nose was still bleeding and my shirt sleeves were about

as soaked as they could get. I yanked up my shirt-front and put it to use.

'Shall we start cleaning this stuff up?' I asked, through the blood and fabric.

'I don't think so,' Doug said, 'I think you should go back to the house and change your shirt. That much blood doesn't look respectable. Consider the feelings of the park users. Clean up.'

I didn't want to leave him. Something in my stomach told me not to. I said, 'I don't like to leave you alone in the middle of this mess.'

Doug opened the door for me. 'Give me a minute,' he said,' 'to be privet. I need to be privet for a moment or two. Get washed up.'

I walked past him, shuffled past him, out through the door.

Ray was in the kitchen, standing next to the oven and peering into a pan. In one hand he held the saucepan's lid, with his other chubby paw he pulled at his bottom lip, yanking it half-way down his chin.

'Ray, Did you see Saleem and Nancy yet?'

Ray – deep in his own thoughts – hadn't heard me come in. He jumped like a scalded cat and dropped the saucepan's lid when I spoke and then managed to frighten himself again with the clatter that it made. He bent down and picked it up.

'Uh, I saw Saleem. She's upstairs. She's searching through Doug's room for evidence.'

'Evidence?'

'Order forms and stuff. Receipts. I think that's what she said.' He stared at me. 'Where did all that blood come from?'

'My nose.'

'Wu got you.'

'Yes.'

'Again.'

'Yes.'

'How's Doug?'

'Not good.'

61

Ray fitted the lid back onto the saucepan. He stared over towards the window. 'I've got loads to do. I want to finish that gatepost this morning and I swore to Doug I'd weed the tennis courts.'

'I think Doug's got bigger things on his mind at present than the tennis courts.'

Ray scratched his beard. I added, 'I also think we should consider telling Nancy not to go to Southend today for any more privet. We both know the park can't afford it.'

Ray leaned his weight against the oven and shifted it, unintentionally, an inch closer to the wall.

'But the problem is,' I said, hoping for some kind of response, 'I don't know if we can really risk antagonising Doug any further. He's already slightly . . . overwrought.' Ray carried on scratching his beard. 'What do you think?'

Ray picked up the roll of kitchen towel and tossed it over to me. 'Have you tried pinching the top of your nose? That might stop it bleeding.'

Saleem came in clutching a folder and a bundle of papers. She threw them on to the table. 'There,' she said, 'I knew he'd started keeping some of this stuff upstairs. He's getting paranoid. Being secretive's a real symptom of it. Right, let's split this lot up between us and see what we can find.'

I looked over towards the door. 'Doug might come back here at any time.'

Saleem smiled, 'We're OK. Nancy's on lookout.'

Ray stayed over by the oven, like he didn't want any part of looking through the papers. Saleem pulled out a chair and placed herself squarely on to it. She began leafing through. 'Pull up a pew, Phil. Take the weight off your bad foot.' I remained standing, breathing into a clump of tissue.

'OK . . . OK . . .' Saleem rifled through the top few sheets. She pulled something out. 'Privet!' she announced, excitedly, 'Bingo!' She passed it over to me. I looked at it. An advance order requesting privet amounting to the sum of fifteen hundred pounds.

Saleem carried on rifling. She said, 'I don't know how the

hell he's intending to explain away this little lot tomorrow at the meeting.'

I looked over at Ray. 'Fifteen hundred pounds,' I said, miserably.

Ray shifted his weight. 'Maybe you should ring them,' he volunteered, 'and tell them we can't actually afford to pay for it.'

'Maybe.'

My head felt weightless. My head felt like the bright-faced bulb of yellow sunflower. All colour, display, no substance. I pulled out a chair and sat down.

'Saleem,' I said, gently, 'I've been thinking about what you said earlier. About Wu not destroying Doug's greenhouse. Because if Wu didn't destroy it, then who did?'

'Vandals.'

'They didn't break in. They had a key.'

'Clever vandals. You're dripping blood on the floor.'

I looked down. Cog had appeared at my feet and was nosing at the drops of blood. His little pink tongue protruded and he started to lap it up. I bent over to push him away and as I bent, my head started rolling and roaring like it was full of buzzing, like it was a fluffy bumble just about to detach itself, to fly off.

It would have flown, I'm sure it would have flown, except for the fact that at that exact moment Nancy burst into the kitchen and yanked me up. She stared into my face. 'Listen,' she said, breathless, 'that's Doug.'

Slowly, I blinked. 'Doug?' I tried to focus on her face but her eyes were everywhere. I tried to focus.

'He's taken the tractor. That's him, outside. Listen.'

Saleem stuffed the papers into the folder, threw the folder into the cutlery drawer, grabbed hold of my arm. 'Outside,' she said, 'come on.'

Actually, we must've looked quite funny, the four of us, standing there in a line, like we were preparing to be presented to the Queen in a formal ceremony. Just outside the gate, near the Ladies toilets, we had a full view of Doug, the tractor, the lakes, the greenhouses, the hill opposite, the whole damn vista.

'Where's he going?' Ray asked. 'Any ideas?'

'Maybe he's thinking about mowing the grass patch just beyond the bandstand,' I suggested. Saleem snorted. Nancy said, 'He doesn't have the mower attachment on the back.'

'Did he say anything?' Ray asked, 'to you?'

Nancy shook her head. 'Nope. Just picked up the heavy-headed axe and climbed into the tractor.'

Ray looked at me. I shrugged.

'This is it.' Saleem said. 'This is the big one.'

'How?' I asked, losing patience, almost.

'I'll bet you any amount he's going to drive that tractor straight into the greenhouse.'

The tractor trundled and grumbled, between the lakes, beyond the lakes.

'He wouldn't do that.'

'Wanna bet?' Saleem put out her hand, palm skywards.

'He wouldn't do that.'

Beyond the lakes, up the hill. I saw the tractor's rear indicator flashing right. Saleem chortled at this. 'My God,' she said, 'he's a one-off. He's fucking *crazy*.'

A sharp, right turn, a questionable gear-change. 'Ouch,' Nancy muttered. And then, a revving, a roaring, a speeding up.

'He's bending down,' Ray said, perturbed, 'not even looking where he's going.'

'I know what he's up to,' Saleem said. 'He's weighing down the accelerator with the axe-head.'

Fifteen foot to go. Ten foot, five. Doug bounced out of the tractor and landed, cat-careful, on all fours, stayed hunched for a moment, stood up. The tractor – 'I told you! I told you' Saleem cackled – slowed down for a moment, choked, stuttered, lurched, kept lurching, until CRUNCH. It hit the main glasshouse, shattering and clattering, bending metal, running, roaring, covering, collapsing. And shards fell from above, the engine cut. More collapsing, more shards, a tiny, silly tinkling, a rumble, a small, metallic burp.

Doug didn't pause to look at or appraise his handiwork. He didn't turn, he kept on walking. 'He's so cool,' Nancy whispered, 'like John Wayne or that other guy with black hair and funny eyes who's in *The Gunfighter*.'

'Gregory Peck,' Ray mumbled.

'That's the one. Yeah.'

A woman in a headscarf who had been walking her miniature collie nearby called out the dog's name harshly and then, when he didn't come to heel, put two fingers between her lips and whistled. And strangely enough, it was that whistle, that sound alone which made my legs shake and my eyes fill, not any of the others. That sound alone.

'Oh shit,' Ray said, 'Doug's heading back this way. I'm off.' Ray scarpered.

Doug was strolling back in the general direction of the house. He was wiping his hands on the seat of his trousers. He seemed extremely interested in the condition of the flowering borders. At one point, I swear it, he stopped and removed a dead flower head.

Saleem turned to me. 'Phil,' she said, gently, 'maybe you should find some rope and cordon the greenhouse off, make sure it's safe before someone gets hurt over there. We'll handle Doug. Between the two of us. Me and Nancy.'

I nodded. I turned. I went to get some rope, a canvas sack, some tape and a large, strong, natural fibred, needle-bristled brush.

It was arduous, it was risky and it took just about forever. I wondered where the hell Ray had got to. I couldn't imagine he was helping Nancy and Saleem with Doug at the house. And he certainly wasn't here, helping me, clearing away the glass and mud and metal and vegetables. More than likely he was on the tennis courts, weeding.

I was almost glad to be alone. Things were moving slowly. I was moving slowly. Like something newly born, inhabiting a fresh and different body; testing out what I could and couldn't do, establishing my limited capabilities.

Luckily the damage to the greenhouse was acute but also clearly defined. After a few hours of sweeping and chipping, of taping up sharp corners, of knocking out half-spent panes, I managed to clamber on to the tractor, clear out some of the glass, pull away the axe-head from the accelerator pedal, straighten out one of the mudguards which had bent and hit its tyre, and then switch on the ignition. Using my dodgy foot, my dodgy arm, I stuck the gears into reverse and roared on out of there.

I looked up nervously, as I reversed. I looked up at the glass ceiling and waited for a reaction, waited for it to shatter and crumble, but nothing happened. It kept its clarity.

And this was the curious part: I had so many other things on my mind – so much to keep in my head – but all the while I felt like everything was flowing. A liquid sensation. Maybe it was the blood in me, travelling through my body, blooming in my face, my cheeks, but then moving on, carrying on, *flowing*. And I should have been thinking and sorting and planning in my head, organizing, controlling, but in fact all I could think of were natural things. Concrete things. Physical substances. *Substance*. Nature. Bark, rock, soil, water.

And gradually I started thinking about water and rock. How they are the two most extreme substances, two opposite poles, and yet, and yet they can work together. They can work together and be together and live together and although they both have their own energy, their own terrible strength and power, at the same time, they do not *violate* each other. Because that's how nature moves, how it works. It cooperates. And that's how I wanted to move – no more smashing and crashing and thumping and punching, I wanted to move like the water around the rock. And that was how I *had* been moving, all along, if only I'd seen it.

'Hey, Phil.'

What was I doing? I was in the greenhouse, standing amid

the wreckage, and I was holding one of Doug's giant onions and gazing at it.

'Nice onion,' Ray said, staring at me quizzically.

I imagined how this onion was inside. Layer upon layer of clean white flesh, containing, enveloping, pure and thorough. A circle. Each layer complete and depending. Each layer sharp and moist and spotless. It was so beautiful.

'Maybe you should sit down for a minute?' Ray took the onion from me and threw it into a wheelbarrow. 'Won't be able to eat that,' he said, regretfully. 'When they get too big they taste all watery. Don't taste of anything, in fact.'

Ray led me outside. My leg and arm had both started to stiffen, and the dried blood inside my nostrils itched like crazy. I sat down for a moment on the grass verge. Ray appraised the tractor. He kicked a wheel. He cleared out some glass from under the pedals.

'Not too bad,' he said, cheerfully, 'doesn't look too bad after its big ordeal.' He stared at me again. 'You should go home for a while. Maybe put your feet up for a couple of hours.'

'Have you been back to the house yet?'

He nodded.

'How's Doug?'

Ray cleared his throat. 'Lying low.'

'What's he doing?'

'I don't know.'

'Actually . . .' I tried to straighten my thoughts out. 'This morning when I found the greenhouse all messed up and I got into that fight with Wu . . .'

'Yeah.'

'Nancy was there. She just appeared from nowhere. And it was six in the morning, a good three hours before she usually gets in for work.'

'Probably out for a run.' Ray said, distractedly, and then added, 'I just weeded the tennis courts.'

My head was throbbing. Ray climbed into the tractor and started up the engine. He pressed his foot down on the accelerator a few times and then put it into gear.

'Climb in,' he yelled. 'I'll give you a lift back to the house if you like.'

'What about this?'

I pointed towards the greenhouse. There was still plenty of work left to be done. Ray waved his giant paw at me. 'I'll park this thing in the barn and then head straight on back.'

I struggled up and clambered on to the passenger seat. I hoped the tractor's vibrating wouldn't start my nose off bleeding again. As a cautionary measure I breathed through my mouth, very gently. While I breathed, I inspected my sleeves and shirt-front which were brown and heavy with dried blood. I scratched at it softly with my thumbnail as Ray and I jerked along, between the lakes, past the museum, past the toilets, a sharp right turn and then into the barn. The fabric was scratchy and hard. Stiff and solid and starched with plasma.

I was too slow. Something was very wrong with my head. I couldn't keep up, keep pace, keep time. I stood in the courtyard for several minutes before I'd accumulated enough energy to even consider going into the house. Instead I stood staring stupidly at the rows of privet bushes, little green sentries standing to attention, properly apportioned. Sharply ranked. I stared at them for a while. Ray had gone. Everything was quiet.

I knew there was something that I should be thinking but I couldn't think it. What was it? Did the privet need watering? I felt the base of one of the pots. Dry, but not too bad. I thought about fetching the hose and giving them a spray. But that wasn't it. I looked around me. There was something else. A *lack*. A space. Something empty. And then it struck me. Nancy. The truck. Gone. Both gone. I turned and headed into the house.

'Saleem? Doug?'

I pushed open the kitchen door. The air smelled damp and sweet and strange. The windows were covered in condensation. On the table, laid out, stretched out, was Cog. On his side. He didn't look his normal self. He wasn't allowed, generally, to sit on the table or to lie on it. I put out my hand to touch him, to nudge him.

'Leave him!'

Saleem was behind me. Then she was next to me and then in front of me. She grabbed hold of Cog and he lay limp as lettuce in her arms. A substantial dishcloth. Boneless.

'What's wrong? What's up with the cat?'

Saleem looked hot and ragged. 'He's dead, stupid.'

'Dead?'

I put out my hand to touch him. Saleem jerked him away, out of reach.

'Don't do that!'

'Why not?'

'It's a bit bloody late to start showing him affection now, Phil. It's not like you ever gave a toss about him when he was alive.'

This was honestly the last thing I could have expected. The cat dead. This hadn't been part of the picture. It didn't connect to anything. I stared at Saleem. 'What happened to him?'

'He died.'

'Just like that? He just died? He's not especially old. Not for a cat.'

Cog seemed irresistible, all limp. I reached out my hand again, just to touch, and this seemed to enrage Saleem. She was spitting angry.

'Phil! Just stop it! You are starting to piss me off so badly. I mean the cat's dead and only now do you start giving a shit about it. That's bloody typical of you. Absolutely bloody typical. And I'm under enormous pressure too. I am. I am! And no one gives a shit about me.' Saleem threw Cog on to the table, tossed aside her stick, yanked out a chair, sat down and burst into tears.

I wished I could die. Just die. Lie down with Cog on the table and expire. Saleem's face was wet and glossy and extremely snotty.

Eventually I said, 'Do you want me to bury him?'

She shrugged sulkily.

'There's an empty flower bed at the back of the house. I could put him in there easily enough.' She shrugged again. 'Only,' I said, nervously, 'I hardly think Nancy or Doug would appreciate seeing him dead. Not just at the moment. They're both quite fond of him. So you and I could bury him and just pretend this hadn't happened for a couple of days.'

Saleem wiped her face on the tablecloth. 'OK,' she said, eventually, 'Go dig a hole. I'll bring him out in five minutes' time.'

I nodded. 'By the way,' I said, 'where is Nancy?'

'Dig the fucking hole, Phil.'

I went. I dug.

So it wasn't much of a burial. I dug the hole. Not too deep because I found it hard to hold the spade and hard to balance and the soil seemed unusually hard, too. True to her word, after five minutes Saleem appeared holding Cog. Her face was dry and clear and she seemed, to all intents and purposes, perfectly cheerful again.

I stood aside. I wondered if I should say anything or whether Saleem herself wanted to say a few words.

'Is that it?' Saleem asked, staring at the hole. 'Sure it's deep enough?'

'I hope so.'

'Fine.' She hopped forward, held Cog over the hole and unceremoniously dropped him in.

'Cover him,' she said and watched as I pushed over the soil. She sniffed her hands. 'Christ,' she said, 'I reckon he's already started stinking. My hands smell like old urine.'

I completed the job in silence. Saleem watched me. She made me feel self-conscious. To distract her I said, 'Where's Doug? In bed?'

'What makes you say that?'

'I just wondered where he was. I wondered how he was.'

'He's gone.'

I froze. 'Gone? Where?'

'I don't know. He just said, "I've had enough. I'm going." I asked him if he'd be back for the meeting tomorrow and he said, "Bugger the meeting." '

'Doug actually said that?'

'Yes.'

'I can't believe he'd say that.'

Saleem's mouth began to tighten at its corners. 'He said it.'

'Did he say where he was going?'

'Nope.'

'D'you think he went back to Mercy's?'

'I shouldn't think so.'

I walked to the barn to put the spade away. As I walked I tried to think where Doug would go. I couldn't imagine him going anywhere. This was his place. He wouldn't leave this place.

I decided to try and ring him at Mercy's. I was standing in the hallway, dialing, when Saleem confronted me.

'Who are you ringing?'

'Mercy.'

'What for?'

'To see if Doug's there.'

Saleem slammed down her hand and cut me off.

'That's stupid,' she said. 'You don't want to get Mercy all worked up.'

I put down the receiver. 'Fine,' I said. 'I know he'll be back tomorrow anyway. He wouldn't miss the meeting. Not for anything.'

Saleem eyed me. 'Just the same . . .'

'What?'

'Couldn't do any harm for you to acquaint yourself with the details of the park business, just in case he doesn't.'

'He will.'

'I'm willing to bet he might not.'

'He will. I know how he is.'

'Even so . . .' Saleem had a couple of folders under her arm, 'best acquaint yourself.'

71

I inhaled deeply. I didn't take the folders. I said, 'You know full well that I can't go to the meeting. That's Doug's job.'

Saleem was growing impatient. 'What will it take,' she asked me, 'to make you realize that you are the only person who can go? It's up to you. Doug isn't coming back. I *know* that. OK? He isn't coming back. It's up to you.'

'Then we'll cancel the meeting.'

'We can't cancel it. Doug's cancelled it twice already. All the details, correspondence, everything, are in here. In the folders. Just *take* them.'

I shook my head. I knew Doug. He was the backbone. An organism couldn't function – couldn't walk or crawl or anything – without a backbone. 'He's coming back,' I said, 'that's all I know.'

Saleem was silent for a minute. Then she said, 'Did you read that book like I told you to? Dr John Sledge. Did you read it?'

'Doug's coming back.'

Saleem pushed her face up very close to mine. 'Phil,' she said gently, 'you saw what Doug did this morning. He took the fucking tractor and he drove it into the greenhouse. You saw him do that, didn't you? With your own two eyes.'

She was right in my face, I side-stepped. She side-stepped. I backed my way into the kitchen. Something was boiling. The air was full of steam. Smelled sweet and ugly.

Saleem followed me into the kitchen. She dumped the folders down on to the table and she went to open a window. I watched her. I took a slow step over towards the door.

'Stay where you are.' She turned. 'I have something to tell you. Something important.' We had the whole table between us.

She sighed. 'OK, so I'd hoped to keep it from you so that you wouldn't get all worked up about it and spoil our chances at the meeting tomorrow . . .' I opened my mouth to speak, but she said, 'Don't say it, Phil. Doug won't be back for the meeting tomorrow. He *won't* be, and I'll tell you why.'

It was still too wet and too warm. I put my hands out and rested them on the back of a chair. I leaned on the chair. On the sideboard were a bundle of papers. On the top of these, a newspaper. It was the previous day's *Guardian*.

'Remember this?' Saleem showed me the *Guardian*. I frowned back at her. 'You know when you came in, before, and I was kind of overwrought?'

I nodded. I think I did.

'Well to be honest with you, I don't give a shit about that fucking cat, and I'm sure you're aware of that fact.'

I nodded again. She pulled out a chair and sat down. She said, 'I'll give it to you straight, Phil.'

The chair was creaking under my weight. I was sweating. Or was I covered in condensation? A pan on the oven was boiling. Water and steam and water and steam.

'Right,' Saleem said, 'now just listen. Nancy was really angry with Doug for sacking her yesterday. I tried to convince her last night that you and Ray would make sure she'd be all right. I told her you'd stand up for her against Doug. Well, unfortunately, she wasn't convinced. She was angry with Doug. She went and destroyed his greenhouse this morning. I suppose she just didn't have any faith in the two of you. And she loves this place as much as we do. You might not believe it, Phil but she does. Anyway, after Doug smashed up the tractor and everything she realized how stupid she'd been. Petty and everything. What a big mistake she'd made. So when Doug got back here she told him what she'd done and she told him she'd done it. I guess her timing wasn't up to much, well, she's already proved that quite conclusively, if her driving is anything to go by.

'Anyhow, Doug literally went wild. He felt terribly betrayed. He was yelling and throwing his fists about and he said he'd destroy the whole damn park. I mean he was just crazy. Even I was scared. Nancy was scared too. She ran to the truck, got out her gun – actually it's more like a starting pistol, I think she uses it when she goes motorcross racing or something – and Doug stopped dead in his tracks, but not for long. After a second Doug lunged at her. Nancy's tough, though. She stepped back, tried to get away, but found herself up flat against the back of her truck. She couldn't step back any further. And Doug was getting closer. And then . . . and then . . .'

Saleem's eyes were as large and round as two plates spinning on the end of two sticks. 'And then she just, kind of, shot him. In the foot. I think it was his foot because he staggered and jumped around on one leg for a while.

'Nancy yanked down the tail of her truck and pushed him inside. I mean it took literally five seconds. Doug was still distracted and slightly off balance. Then she closed the back gate. Doug was locked in there. I tried to ask her what she thought she was doing but it all happened so quickly. She just said, "He won't do this to us. He's not going to bully us any more. I'm taking him away. I'm going to keep him locked in there until he sees sense. As long as it takes." Then she jumped into her cab, started up the engine and drove off. And that was that.'

I stared at the window, the point just behind Saleem's right shoulder. Drips of condensation were making patterns on its surface. I wondered what the patterns meant.

'Say something.'

I shook my head. My wet head. I couldn't believe Nancy would behave so stupidly. I closed my eyes. I opened my eyes. The drips on the window spelled the word *muddy*. I blinked. It was gone. I said, 'Nancy wouldn't do something as stupid as that.'

'But you would say that, wouldn't you?'

'What?'

Saleem's lips were thin and white. 'Yeah. You know what I mean.'

She had lost me, finally.

'Saleem, I don't know what you're talking about.'

She leaned her elbows on the table. Her small breasts were squeezed together between her arms. 'Say that again, go on.'

'Say what?'

'My name.'

Saleem. *Saleem*. I couldn't say it. When I said her name it felt like a mouthful of unripe elderberries. On my palate. In my throat.

'Look,' I said, 'I just don't understand why Nancy . . . I need to have it explained again.'

Saleem started to smile. She was a different person, suddenly. She cocked her head to one side. 'I've been giving this some thought,' she said, 'and I don't think it's really a question of understanding, but more an issue of . . . of managing.'

'How?'

'Because it isn't such a bad thing that Doug's out of harm's way for a while. If Nancy keeps him until Friday then you can go to the meeting and everything can take its course after that. Once we're secure. The rest doesn't matter.'

'But what about Nancy?'

Saleem shrugged. 'She'll cope.'

'And Doug?'

'He'll be fine. He just needs a little time away from this place. A little distance.'

'I can't go to the meeting.' I nearly choked saying it. Just saying it was bad enough.

'You have to.'

'I couldn't do it. Doug handles that kind of thing. That's the whole point of him.'

'Let me put it this way,' Saleem said, grinning, 'either you go to the meeting or I'm going to call the police and tell them what I've told you and that will fuck up Nancy very badly indeed. And after I fuck up Nancy I'm going to think of a way to fuck you up.'

'Nancy's in trouble no matter what you do.'

'Who's in trouble?'

'What do you mean?'

'Nancy. Nancy. Whenever you say her stupid name your cheeks go red.'

'That's ridiculous.'

'That's fighting talk.'

'It's not.'

75

'You're making me angry, Phil.'

'I'm not. I'm only trying to understand what's gong on.'

'Some hope, lard-arse.' Saleem jumped up, tossed the paper over towards me, grinned, and scuttled out.

I stared down at the paper. Outlined in blue ink, two headlines. My eyes turned immediately to the second headline. The second headline said: 100-DAY PROTEST.

I read it again, re-acquainted myself with the story of how Mr Peter Hawes had locked himself inside his roadside café. As a protest. Surely it was different though, I decided, surely it was very different to *lock yourself*. Locking yourself was quite the opposite of *being locked*, forcibly.

I tried to picture Doug, being locked, in my mind, but I couldn't picture it. Doug. Where was he? I couldn't picture him. Not at all. Where was he? Doug? Where was he? Suddenly my brain was empty. I knew it, then. Doug was gone. Yes, Doug was lost. Lost.

I found Ray in the greenhouse. 'Ray,' I said, 'things are a mess.'

'Let's go sit on the bench.'

It was Ray's favourite bench, under a yellow laburnum. We sat down.

'OK,' Ray said, 'what needs to be done?' He plucked a couple of seeds from the branches overhead and cracked them open.

'Leave those alone, Ray. They're poisonous.'

He dropped the seeds and wiped his hands on his overalls.

I stared at him for a moment. I wondered what kinds of things were going on in his head. I said, 'So you know about Nancy and Doug?' Ray inspected his fingernails. 'Then why didn't you tell me earlier?'

Ray's jowls descended. He scratched his nose. He said, 'This never would've happened if it wasn't for Nancy's eye.'

'Nancy's eye?'

Ray nodded. 'She lost the use of it in a motorcross accident. Before Christmas. Her right eye. That's why she keeps having accidents. She thinks if she loses this job she won't ever work again. I kind of knew for a while but I hoped it'd sort itself out. I mean, she was desperate, you know?'

Things were shifting. Shifting and moving. 'Ray,' I said, almost cracking, almost splitting like the laburnum pod between his podgy fingers. 'Ray,' I said, 'don't tell me anything else. Let's just concentrate on these three things. One, we need to find Doug. Two, we need to sort things out between Doug and Nancy. Three, we need to make sure that the meeting on Friday passes off all right.'

'And the Chinaman?'

I blinked. 'Best leave him well alone.'

'And Saleem?'

'Saleem?' I almost choked. Ray leaned back, locked his hands over his belly. The bench creaked.

And I looked at Ray, and I looked at my shirt, and I looked at my hands and I looked at my feet. And I looked up. This park. This park was my place and now it had been stolen.

This park, even yesterday, was only soil and plants and weather. A sum of its simple constituent parts. Now it was people and thoughts and concoction. It had been violated. Or else, like Saleem had said, there are events and then there are interpretations of events. I was removed. I was always removed. The park was never mine after all. I was in my head and I was out of it.

I had been plucked like a weed.

MY FOOT WAS SORE but I was walking anyway. I needed to re-acquaint myself. Re-acquaint myself. To look. To touch. To reaffirm how it was that I felt about this place. To get it back. I should have talked to Ray, I should have seen what Ray had to say, but I just didn't, I just couldn't.

This is a physical world. Everything's out there and you can touch it if you want to. You can touch it if you doubt it. Just stretch out your hands and your fingers.

I was walking around the park's perimeter. I was going to feel and identify every single object and particle that I had contributed to this place. I was going to see myself, my face and features in every cowering flower, in every bird and every bud.

In the scented garden where I'd planted the pinks and the jasmine, I swung out my arm and rubbed my hand into lavender. I pinched some mint between my thumb and forefinger, then dabbed my finger on to my tongue. I could taste this place. I could touch it. I could smell this place. I could see it.

I kept on walking. Through the wild part where the squirrels dart. Through the adventure playground where the children run and bound and kid around.

Then I doubled back. To the right, past the ornamental pond. I'd filled that pond. I'd emptied it. I'd cleared out the sweet wrappers and the coins and the cans.

Up and along. The stones I was walking on. The loose gravel. I had laid down that gravel. With these two hands.

And up and up the hill. The giant oak. I had pruned that oak. A large rose bed near the fence. I had chosen those roses. Yellow roses and apricot roses. I had sprayed those roses, I had watered and fed them.

At the hill's crest I found the silver birch and the poplar. I knew how the bark of each tree felt on the calloused palms of my hands and also, and also, on the softer lid of each fist; that bare little space between my fist and my wrist.

And the grass. I had cut it. And the daisies. I had cut them too. And the weeds. I had plucked them out.

Where was the sun? I looked up for it, into the sky. I turned on the spot and tried to see it. It was behind the giant cedar, tucked like a lost ball in its branches. How late was it? The sun made me blink, I closed my eyes and it stayed nestled inside my lids, glaring balefully into my head.

I sat down. My face was damp with sweat. I licked my lips and it was like my tongue had been dipped in the Adriatic. My eyes were still closed but the sun was fading now, flickering inside me.

I put down my hands flat on to the grass. I could feel the soil through the grass. I dug my nails into it.

Doug. Why had the feel of this soil stopped meaning enough? Doug wanted things to be bigger. He wanted something universal. He wanted the colour of the peonies, the height of the pampas grass, the smell of the honeysuckle to mean something. And did it mean something? And should it?

I opened my eyes. Doug had slipped in, into my head. Doug and his doings, Saleem and her words, Nancy and her muddy hands, Ray and his *insight*, all of these things were pulling me away from what I should be thinking about, from what I should be believing in. The soil. The sun. The shade. The bright glow of the buttercup.

I turned and looked down at the park below me, all its parts fitting together. And my nose was itching and my eyes were smarting and something or someone was knocking on the inside of my skull. Knock, knock. Knock, knock. Trying to attract my attention.

And how was I feeling? How was I doing? What was I thinking? Who did I believe? Oh *Christ*. I'm so sick of this head. So sick of this head. I'm sick of it. I am. Sick.

I sat on the grass, on the slope. I wanted to be simple, a natural part of the landscape but my mind wouldn't let me. I stretched out my legs. I pulled up my trouser and inspected my ankle. It had swollen out of the top of my sock. It had swelled like pale, prime dough out of my shoe and was glooping over my laces. It was pale as cooked fish-flesh, though, and felt numb when I pinched it.

I rolled up my sleeve and inspected my arm. It still had its bruises, but now it was bent too, curved in the strangest places like a finely crafted piece of metal piping. Some new, pinky marks were dawdling up near my elbow. My shoulder smarted a little. I picked out some of the dry blood from my nostrils. That, at least, was satisfying.

While I picked I looked down at the park. Dumbly, duti-fully. I looked through the trees, the tall grass, past the roses, the flower beds, the pond. And there, sitting next to the pond, I could have sworn I saw a cat. A big tabby, licking its tail.

Could I trust my eyes? I clambered up and started to walk, down the hill. The slope made me trot, made me jog. At the bottom of the slope I carried on jogging: through the trees, the flower beds, up to the water.

Cog rolled on to his back and offered me his belly. I squatted down, panting. I rubbed it. As I rubbed a small sprinkle of mud and dust rose and fell. Then Cog stood up and sauntered off, his little jaunty bollocks to the rear, neat and well balanced like a sprig of cherries.

It was then that I decided to be someone else. Seeing the cat, like that, resurrected. It was so curious. Could I be someone else? Temporarily? Could I be someone else, altogether?

I crawled over to the edge of the pond. I saw my face in it. My face looked different. Swollen at its gills, wild-eyed. My cheeks were scratched like I'd had a tangle with a fistful of thorns.

Who was I? Who could I be? I didn't care. I'd be anyone. Anyone at all. I'd even forgo the thrill of being someone else so long as I was not my self. Was it possible?

Yes. I could be. I could be un-Phil. Out-of-Phil. Un-fool-Philled. Yes.

And the process was a simple one. To scrape out a gap in my gut like the pond. Water in the middle. Rock on the edges. Water flowing. Rock, holding in, containing, not hurting. This sublime pool inside me and a chalk-empty mind. No thought, only pure action. No doubt, only purpose. The three Ps. Park (my heart), Pond (my gut), Purpose (alone).

Park, pond, purpose.

Park, pond, purpose.

Park, pond, porpoise.

My brain rattled like a chickpea inside my skull.

THERE WAS BLOOD on the courtyard. Was it Doug's or was it mine? Some stains near the privet. An unsightly little brown rivulet. Only sap, I told myself, just red, not green.

I pushed at the front door but it would not open. It had been locked from inside. I rang the bell. After a short wait, Saleem answered.

'What?'

'Can I come inside for a moment?'

'No. I'm busy. I'm cleaning. I've washed the kitchen floor. I don't want your muddy footprints all over it.'

I didn't baulk or shirk. I was empty-Phil. She couldn't touch me. 'I just saw the cat, Saleem.'

'So?'

I didn't hesitate, not for a second. 'I just saw the cat by the pond, large as life. You said he was dead.'

'So what's the big deal?'

'We just buried him.'

Saleem raised her eyebrows. 'So?'

'You said that the cat was dead and so we buried him.'

She scratched her nose, 'As I recall, I never actually said we should bury the cat. That wasn't my idea.'

Everything flowing. I told myself, everything flows. 'Saleem, you said the cat was dead.'

'I might've said that the cat was *tired*. I might conceivably have said that.'

She was either very funny or she was mad. Or else she was truly evil and she wanted to hurt me. She could kill with one flash of her eye. She smelled of pepper. She was wearing a wellington boot, a pair of old overalls, the spare leg tied up, fastened with a safety pin but still dangling.

Pool, pond, purpose, I told myself. That wasn't right. It didn't work. It didn't flow, not properly. The serene lake in my gut began leaking. Saleem was filling my stomach with lies. Her tongue was a spade and she shovelled them out, out of her mouth and into my ears. Her tongue was heaped with falsehood and fallacy.

Saleem was about to close the door when I stopped her with my hand. And very bravely, very proudly I said, 'You're just like an owner with a ball.'

'What?' She scowled at me.

'You know, when an owner throws a ball for his dog and the dog goes and fetches the ball and brings it back? And after a while the owner gets bored of the throwing and the retrieving so he pretends to throw the ball and he doesn't actually throw it, but the dog's so stupid that it runs for what it thinks is the ball anyway. Even though there's nothing there. Just thin air.'

She carried on scowling, 'You've got it wrong,' she said. 'You mean the boy who cried wolf. That's the fable.'

I shook my head. My brain rattled. 'No. Not that story. This is a different one. In this story, the next time the owner throws the ball he does actually throw it and the dog still appears to have faith in him because he runs just as readily, except, this time, when the dog returns with the ball and the owner reaches out his hand to take the ball away, this time, the dog won't hand it over. He clamps his jaws together. He won't give it up. He's making his feelings clear about the little deception of earlier. That's all.'

Saleem's expression turned from derision to perplexity. 'Phil,' she said, 'I think you might be a little concussed. You're babbling.'

I was sad again and vulnerable again but I was still determined. 'No. I'm making perfect sense.'

'You're talking shit, Phil. It sounds like perfect sense to you because your head has taken a knocking, but in fact it's only drivel. Trust me on this one. Wait a minute.'

Saleem closed the door and left me on the doorstep for a short duration. When she reappeared she was clutching a couple of folders, a carrier bag and her front door keys.

'I'm going to take you home.'

'I don't want to go home. I want to talk to Ray.'

'I can't think Ray'll want to talk to you right now. You're nonsensical. Come on. Home. Walk with me.'

Saleem grabbed hold of my bad arm and she yanked it. It felt like it might snap. It groaned, the way a big ship groans and whines when it's being launched for the very first time. I gave in and staggered along beside her.

'We've got to calm that brain of yours down a little bit,' she said, as she walked. 'This place is like a sodding war zone.'

'You don't see the plants and the grass and the trees fighting,' I said, trying to get back my previous state of equilibrium, 'only people.'

'Say another stupid thing like that,' Saleem whispered, 'and I'll put my fucking fist in your mouth.'

I'd imagined things would feel better horizontal but I was wrong. I was flat on my back, on my sofa. My feet and ankles were slung up and over the arm. Saleem had insisted that I lie this way. It was extremely uncomfortable. Saleem herself was in my kitchen, cooking.

'I'm going to feed you and feed you,' she yelled through the kitchen's open doorway, 'till your stuffed up like a rooster.'

After ten minutes she came through holding a tray. On the tray was a plate which was full of a brown, glutinous substance, slightly fried. 'Sit up and eat this shit.'

I sat up, dutifully. 'What is it?'

'It's brain food.'

'Aren't you having any?'

'Only enough there for one serving, you lucky devil.'

Saleem handed me the plate and a fork. I sliced into the brown stuff and swallowed a mouthful. It had a meaty, metallic taste to it. I ate another mouthful. I chewed briefly and swallowed. 'Is this liver?' I asked, forking up some more.

Saleem grinned, 'Nope.'

'It tastes like liver.'

Saleem scratched the tip of her stump and hopped over to peruse a photograph on the mantelpiece of my dead aunt with my dead grandparents posing on the beach at Southend.

'Remember this morning?' she asked, her back to me, 'when you got dragged in by Nancy and your nose started bleeding?'

'Yes.'

'Remember when Doug came down and you had that giant piece of jelly dangling from your nose?'

'Yes.'

'At the time if kind of reminded me of black pudding. While I watched you pull it out I wondered how it would taste if it was gently fried.'

I stopped chewing. I put down my plate and hobbled into the kitchen. I threw up into the sink. I turned on the tap and washed the mush I'd produced down the plug-hole. I poured myself a glass of water and returned to the living room.

Saleem was still staring at the picture. 'But then it dawned on me,' she said, as though there hadn't been any hiatus in our conversation, 'that black pudding is a mixture of pig's blood and fat. Plain blood, if heated, would probably just disintegrate. The fat'd be the thing that would hold it together.'

I stared at her. I said, 'You are a very sick, very cruel person.'

She turned and smiled. 'Cool, calm, confident,' she said. 'The three Cs, remember?'

I sat down and pressed my glass of water up against my hot head.

'Events,' she added, 'and how you choose to *interpret* events. Two totally different kettles of fish, like I told you.' I said nothing. 'You've got a whole lot of work to do in that department, Phil. You're too bloody suggestible. And you always seem determined to think the very worst of other people. I mean, I've come into your home and I've fried you the kidneys I was intending to cook for my own dinner. A selfless act. But still you manage to convince yourself that I mean you harm. Is that an entirely acceptable, a reasonable way to be thinking?'

I held my glass of water in front of me and stared at it.

'You are the exact same person,' I said, 'who got me to bury a live cat in the garden a few hours ago.' Before she could respond I added, 'And Doug drove his tractor into the greenhouse. Then he threatened Nancy. And Nancy, Nancy wrecked Doug's vegetables and then shot Doug in the foot with a starting pistol before kidnapping him in the back of her truck.'

I looked up and over my glass and stared into Saleem's eyes. 'And you think I've been hasty in judging everyone? You really think I'm always determined to see the worst in people?'

Saleem grimaced. 'Your problem is that you don't think a person has any right to be more complicated than a fern or a bloody chrysanthemum. People live much more complicated lives than plants, Phil.'

'I don't think that way at all. Not at all.'

'Yes, you do.'

'No, I don't.'

'Christ, you've become argumentative since you bumped your head. Let's hope this'll mean that you're extremely persuasive and forthright at the meeting tomorrow.'

I lay down on the sofa again. I was tired now. I closed my eyes. Saleem came and stood over me. She said, 'Finish your kidneys. You need some energy. You've got to take a good look at those files. You've got to assimilate all the receipts and the documents.'

'I don't want the kidneys. I don't care about the files.'

Although my eyes were tightly shut I could feel Saleem right up close to me. When she next spoke I felt her breath on my ear and on my cheek.

'Are you telling me,' she whispered, 'that the park means so little to you that this, the tiniest of sacrifices, is too much for you to make? The possibility of even the smallest bit of effort and discomfort are enough to make you abandon everything? Everyone?'

But it wasn't that. The park meant too much, not too little. How could I be held responsible for something that I loved so completely? 'Find Doug and let him go,' I said, somewhat unreasonably. 'Let Ray go,' I added, 'or go yourself if you feel that strongly about it. I don't care who goes. I won't go.'

Saleem was silent for so long that I opened one of my eyes and peeped out at her to check that she was still there. She was there. The air was bare with glare and stare. She was there.

'And you dare to tell me,' she gurgled, finding her voice, at last, locating it in the guttural regions of her lower throat, 'and you *dare* to suggest to me that I wouldn't sacrifice everything for something that I loved?'

'That's not what I was saying at all.'

'You dare to suggest that?'

Suddenly fearful, I said, 'It's a question of caring too much, not too little, that's what I'm saying. It's all right if someone else destroys the one thing you love most in the world but its a terrible thing if you destroy it yourself. No feeling could be worse than that.'

'You're wrong.' Saleem was still gurgling. 'You're wrong, Phil. What you can't see is that it's better to destroy the thing you love than to have it snatched away from you. I've learned that lesson and Doug's learned that lesson. Even Nancy's learned it. But not you.'

I shook my head. She ignored my shaking.

'When they told me they were refurbishing the museum and turning it into a crèche and a café,' she murmured, lethally, 'when they told me they wouldn't be needing a curator any more, I didn't just walk away.' I opened my eyes again. She grinned. 'I didn't just walk away. I lost my leg in that fire. And after the fire, no one could take away the books and the pictures and the papers. No one could take them away. And look where I locked them . . .' Saleem patted her left breast with her right hand. 'My heart. And that's a very tight, very dark, very *secure* place.'

I stared at her blankly. She stood up. 'Finish your kidneys,' she said, and then she picked up her stick and left me.

I RAN A WARM BATH and soaked every bit of me in it. I stuck my head underwater and breathed the water in through my nose, swallowed some of it, blew the rest of it out, full of soil and muck and flaking red residue.

After the bath I had hoped to feel bolder, but I didn't. I looked in the mirror and saw the same hairy, scared creature staring straight back at me.

In my bedroom I pulled on a clean shirt and some trousers. I pulled out my suit too, my funeral suit, from the back of the wardrobe, and laid it flat across the bed. My funeral suit. Whose funeral? I put the suit away again.

Still on the pillow lay Dr John Sledge's *I'm Not Angry, I'm Hurting*. I picked it up. I opened it. At the top of the page was a heading in bold lettering. It said: WHAT HAVE YOU GOT TO LOSE?

Everything or nothing? Think about it for a moment. Give this question some serious thought, and once you have thought about it, think about this:

(1) If you've got A LOT to lose, then why take the risk of losing it? If you've got A LOT to lose then you've got something worth fighting for.

(2) If you've got NOTHING to lose, then why delay? Act today. What possible harm could it do you? Things can only get better. You've got NOTHING to lose and everything to gain.

Repeat after me, out loud, 'I've got nothing to fear but fear itself.' Again, 'I've got nothing to fear but fear itself.' Feeling better? Well done. Why am I congratulating you? I'll tell you why. I'm congratulating you because you are on the road to healing yourself. It's a wonderful journey. Come, travel with me.

I shut the book, turned it over and stared at the photograph of Dr John Sledge on the back of it. Dr Sledge was younger than I imagined. He had a head like a pumpkin. He exuded a kind of ghastly, glistening rude health. He had a mole in between his nose and his top lip. He was smiling broadly and he had perfect teeth. Out loud I said it. 'Dr Sledge,' I said, 'if you came and sat down next to me on a train I'd change compartments.'

I brewed some coffee. I ate three pieces of bread and butter. While I ate I considered the things I had yet to do. Some strimming by the rose garden, the hydrangeas needed cutting back. I'd noticed some of the rubbish bins by the tennis courts were full. What else? Nothing else.

I searched for my keys, found them, picked up a jumper from the back of a chair because the air outside had turned nippy. As I picked up the jumper I knocked the files which Saleem had balanced precariously on the edge of the kitchen table. I swore. The top one fell and the bottom one followed. Their paper guts scattered across the floor. And as I picked up each sheet I told myself: See this? All this writing and planning and calculating? This is the business, this stuff. The park, well that's something altogether different. They are two different entities. Altogether separate.

But the paper was covered in Doug's close hand. Doug's figures and letters. I couldn't help but see Doug in these papers. I picked them up. Some had doodles on them, inkspots, drops of tea, bits of crumb. Some were crumpled, others pristine. Some were stuck together. I tried to pull these apart as a tribute to Doug and then there, before me, the most incredible thing happened.

The paper unfolded. Several sheets had been stuck together with Sellotape, hinged together on purpose. I unfolded, one piece and two pieces, three pieces, four, and beheld the most perfect, most detailed, accurate and lovely sketch, in green and red pen – mad colours – of the park: all its parts, but something new, too.

In gorgeous detail, a little maze. A magical thing. A heart-shaped maze with a waterfall at its centre. Ornate statues in dead ends, occasional arches and trellises, and honeysuckle. Spy-glasses and sunflowers and poppies growing through the privet. Concrete frogs peeping out from corners and pheasants stalking with glass tails.

And at last, I saw Doug. I saw Doug. My hands started shaking, my eyes filled, because at last I saw Doug. He was right there in front of me. He was not lost any more.

I FORGOT ABOUT ALL those other tasks. Instead I stared at Doug's plans for what seemed like an eternity. Of course he's mad, I told myself. Of course he is. And when I told myself that Doug was mad it sounded in my ears like the grandest kind of compliment, an accolade, the sweetest benediction.

Once I'd familiarized myself thoroughly with every detail of Doug's crazy plan, I read through the other stuff too. I put the receipts into some semblance of order, I calculated how much we'd spent over the last year and on what, and how much we'd saved by frugal management. I tried to work out whether we could claim for the damage to the greenhouse under our present system of insurance. And then I went out.

I went out and I walked for a very long time. Things needed sorting and I wasn't entirely sure who was going to sort them. Was I going to sort them? Could I?

I walked for a very long time and eventually I found myself in Southgate and I was outside an all-night chemist and then I was inside and standing by the counter.

'Can I help you?' He was a young man with ginger hair and brown eyes. He wore a white lab coat and glasses. I said, 'I want a packet of condoms please. Extra small.'

Slightly surprised, he pointed to my left. 'Over there, on the counter. We have several varieties. All sizes.'

I said, 'Only sometimes it's hard to find the extra small ones because . . . they're extra small.' My face was a fire engine.

'I'll help you look, shall I, sir?'

Cool, calm, collected. Breathe one, breathe two, breathe three. 'That's kind of you. Thanks.'

My voice was going. I sounded Scottish, to myself; vowels crawling out from all corners of my mouth like crabs.

He rummaged for a while and produced three different packets.

'Three types. Any preference?'

'Any. All. I'll take all three. Thank you.'

'I'll pop them in a bag for you, shall I, sir?'

'Grand. Thanks.'

'There we go.'

'Thanks. Very much.'

You see, the problem is a very simple one, really. It's all a question of wanting – not just wanting, but *needing*, like something categorical. Needing to be a part of a landscape. It's about belonging to a place and wanting to belong and not knowing whether other people will even let you get around to *feeling* like you belong.

It's more than that, more even than that. It's like wanting to be an *actual*, a *physical* part of the landscape.

Animals do it. A bird belongs to the sky and the trees just as much as the trees and the sky themselves belong. No one questions – no one thinks to question – whether the worm a bird plucks from the soil is rightfully his. How could a berry belong anywhere else but in a starling's gut? No one doubts it.

But people. Where do we fit in? How can we fit in? How do we know that we fit and who can we ask? And some people will always feel like they fit and try to make others feel like they don't. And others won't ever fit or feel like they fit, will never, ever feel that way.

All these thoughts, every single one of them, were my technique for avoiding stuff that was happening, that would happen. And I wouldn't stop it. I couldn't stop it.

I'd asked for the condoms, hadn't I? Saleem was right. Maybe the only way to stop being embarrassed was to no longer avoid it. To search it out, to try – even – to enjoy it. To embrace it.

I walked for a very long time and then I got on a bus and ended up in Enfield outside an all-night chemist. And then I was inside the chemist and I was telling the assistant – a small, dark woman with a silver moustache – I've got crabs. Do you have anything for crabs? Are there many different varieties of crab? What are mine like? I don't know. Little ginger things, tiny things.

I caught another bus, stayed on it, ended up in Wood Green. A young woman was in the chemist's, an attractive young woman with red lips and black eyes.

Cool, calm, confident.

'I want some tampons for my mother. It's an emergency.'

'Any particular kind? There are several varieties.' She pointed.

'Which are the good ones?'

'Tampax, Li-lets. They're all OK.'

'Regular, medium-flow, light-flow? Oh God.'

'Why don't you get regular. That's a fairly safe bet.'

'Is it?'

'I think so.'

'She didn't say.'

'Well, it's entirely up to you.'

'Maybe she'd prefer one of those padded things.'

'A towel.'

'Yes, maybe a trowel.'

'*Towel.*'

'Pardon?'

'You said "trowel".'

'Oh, sorry.'

'You might be better off in a hardware store.' She was laughing.

'Sorry. You probably think I'm an idiot.'

'It doesn't matter what I think. Your mother's the one who's having the crisis.'

'I'm the one having a crisis.'

'Know the feeling.'

'You do?'

'Sure.'

'I'll have the regular tampons. You're right.'

'Fine.'

She grabbed them and bagged them. I paid for them.

'You've done the rounds tonight,' she said, pointing at the other two bags I was holding, smiling.

I was beyond blushing. Hot and red and hot and red and

hot and hot and hot and red. It didn't matter any more. Things were too bad. I shook my head, 'I'm just a wanker.'

'Right. Fine.' She shrugged and laughed.

'Thanks.'

'It was nothing.'

Almost ten o'clock. I stood by the bus stop, blinded by the fluorescent lights from the Shopping City, bemused by the concrete everywhere, the red-brick, glass, plastic, all those other city things. I imagined the soil underneath the shopping complex, flattened down hard and close by the weight of the city above; crushed, compacted, useless, like the core of a bad molar. And the city's breath, flowing in and out of its rotting mouth, warm with fumes and dark and stinking.

No buses, not for a while. I started walking. I had a blister on the side of my foot. My shoes weren't the problem, only the fact that I was placing my bad foot and ankle differently when I hobbled and so making the leather rub.

Past Top Rank Bingo, past Wood Green Tube Station, past the bus garage, past the town hall, past the church and on and along. I'd seen teeth on the pavement outside The Tottenham once – a pub painted in pastel shades but its bland colour was deceptive – so crossed over before I reached it, to the other side where Fagin's Talk of the Town Nightspot was bumping and grinding, its disco lights bleaching and bloodying the pavement, its music leaking out too, into the night air.

If I hadn't crossed over I wouldn't have seen it. If my foot hadn't been smarting I wouldn't have paused to adjust my shoe. But I did stop and I did see it. Parked down the side of Fagin's, half in the shade, half lit by a streetlight, a Daf Roadrunner, white, in good condition, Truck of the Year in God knows when.

I went and took a closer look. Could I remember the registration? I couldn't remember it. I almost walked away and then I noticed the front indicator, on the left. It had been smashed.

I ran to the back door and tried to open it. Locked, I knocked

94

on the tailgate. No sound. I pressed my ear up close to its cool metal and held my breath, but nothing was audible from within.

Fagin's. Legendary Nightspot of North London. Above the entrance, a snot-green, life-sized, brass statue of Fagin himself – a skinny, untrustworthy looking character in a stetson, guitar slung across his shoulder, holding up two fingers in a weak-limbed sign of peace.

I didn't want to go in but I went in anyway. Five pounds on the door. Red strobes lit up and picked out a small gaggle of people nestled inside intimate, velvet-coated cubicles. No Nancy. A clutch of characters were cradling their drinks by the bar. No Nancy. Three people were on the dance floor, clumping gracelessly, careful not to make eye contact with each other or with me while their mouths silently worked on the lyrics to the song that was playing. *Ain't no stopping us now. We're on the move! Ain't no stopping us now. We're in the groove!*

I squinted around me, looking for Nancy but not seeing her. I described her in some detail to the barman. He was giving most of his attention to changing the optic on a bottle of Malibu. When I persisted he shrugged and shook his head. 'I only just came on my shift, mate.'

I bought a drink but didn't drink it. I left it on the bar and headed for the exit, past the toilets and the cloakroom and the coat-check girl. I stopped in my tracks and doubled back. 'Excuse me,' I said, and described Nancy to her. The girl winked. 'Have you got a ticket?'

'Pardon?'

'A ticket.' She put out her hand and grinned. She had a tight, high ponytail on the top of her head which made her look like a pineapple, and wide-spaced teeth. She was a Martian.

'I don't have a ticket.'

The girl was still grinning. She said, 'Well, the policy is that if you want to collect something then you have to exchange a ticket for it. I mean, you could be anybody. How am I supposed to tell that the item in question is actually yours?'

Using her thumb, she indicated over her shoulder to where a small collection of summer jackets were hung on numbered metal hangers. I stared at the coats blankly.

The girl tossed her head and her hair nearly took out my eye. 'Not there, stupid! On the floor.'

I looked down. Huddled in an ungainly heap against the wall, half covered in a denim jacket, apparently sleeping – eyes shut – but still making the kind of quiet retching noises a cat makes after it's devoured a gutful of grass: Nancy.

'How long has she been there?'

'Since she got pissed and passed out by the bar.'

'Is she all right?'

'What do you reckon, Einstein?'

The girl unlocked the kiosk and beckoned me inside. 'Take her away with you before she chucks up in here.'

'Nancy?' I crouched down next to her and touched her shoulder. 'Nancy? Wake up.'

Very slowly, Nancy opened her right eye and stared at me.

'Nancy, it's me. Phil.'

Not a glimmer of recognition. The coat-check girl came and stood beside me. I said, 'I don't think she even knows who I am.'

The girl stared intently into Nancy's face. 'Nah, she'll be OK, it's her bad eye, that's all. The right one. She just can't see you from that side.' She nudged Nancy's shoulder, 'Come on, you. It's home time.'

Nancy had been blind in one eye since before Christmas and this was the first time I'd actually noticed, and yet Pineapple Head had observed and digested it seemingly in a matter of moments. I stared up at her with new regard. 'How did you know? About her eye, I mean.'

The girl adjusted her ponytail and said, 'I noticed when she checked in her coat. I put the ticket down on the counter, just to the right of her and she didn't seem to see it.'

I stared deep into Nancy's right eye and saw that it was pure and glassy. And I suddenly felt almost tearful. That dead right eye gave me the strangest sensation – like my feelings, my feelings and fact, *fact*, were two totally separate things. My feelings and fact. I was deluded.

My mind turned to Doug and what he'd said in the greenhouse that morning. *If you can't trust your instincts, what can you trust?* I stared down at Nancy. What is there to a person, after all, beyond how they feel? What are human beings apart from little bundles of feelings and apprehensions and misapprehensions?

Nancy started wheezing more violently.

'Out!' the coat-check girl yelled, 'before she hurls. Quick!'

'Nancy.' I shook her shoulder, harder this time, 'Hey, Nancy, wake up.'

Very slowly, very gradually, Nancy opened her other eye. Wide and then wider.

'Phil!' she mumbled, speaking like her tongue had trebled in size and was working on inhabiting the whole of her head. Her right eye stared through me, the left eye skittered and slid around.

'Hello Nancy. Where's Doug?'

She turned her head, 'Doug? Where?'

'Yes.'

She eyed me expectantly. I stared back, for a moment, before it dawned on me that she wasn't intent on telling but on waiting for an answer. I said, 'Isn't he still in your truck?'

'I'm sorry,' Nancy muttered, woozily, 'all the veg-e-ta-bles.' After a short pause she added, 'Boom! Just like Gregory Peck. Boom!' She cackled and made pathetic little mushroom-shaped cloud pictures in the air with her hands.

I peered up at the coat-check girl again. 'Do you remember by any chance whether she arrived here alone or with someone else? A man.' The coat-check girl was no longer feeling quite as cooperative as before. 'She could've come in with seventeen eunuchs and a Jack Russell for all I care. I want her out of here.'

Nancy's eyes were closing again. 'Come on,' I said, and grabbed hold of her arm. I tried to tug her up but wasn't strong enough.

'Out of my way, you twat,' the coat-check girl clucked, pushing me aside, bending from the knee, lifting Nancy up with apparent ease and draping her across her shoulder. 'I'll take her down the corridor to the public phone and then it's up to you,' she declared tartly, and led the way.

The cab driver stared at Nancy and said, 'If she spews in my car I'll make you lick up every last drop of it.'

I gave him Ray's address and then spent the entire journey staring at Nancy's mouth and her throat, waiting for her to retch, waiting to catch any liquid in my cupped hands or in the flaps of my shirt-front.

Nancy didn't seem to know what she was doing or where she was going. She lay across my lap and panted like an old dog pants when the sun has risen to its midday height and the shade he was lying in has crept a short distance away, but he's too old and too tired to drag his stiff bones back into it. She panted in just that way, but thank God she did not retch. I still tried talking, though. 'Doug,' I kept asking, 'where did you put him? Is he still in your truck? Was he bleeding?' 'Mine's a Bacardi,' she rasped, 'with coke and ice.'

Once we'd arrived, the driver didn't want to help me with Nancy but he didn't have much choice. She had to be moved and I wasn't man enough to move her. He dumped her on Ray's doormat. She grinned up at him, gratefully, while he overcharged me.

Ray answered the door wearing an old striped night-shirt that reached just below his knees. He looked like a waxen and buttery Wee-Willie-Winkie.

'So you found Nancy, then,' he said, sounding not the slightest bit surprised, picking her up and tossing her like a bag of compost over his shoulder. I followed him upstairs, into his flat. He threw her face down on to his sofa. She pushed her nose into a pillow and wheezed.

'How about Doug?' Ray asked, 'Did you find him too?'

'Nope.'

He looked down at Nancy. 'Did she tell you anything?'

'Too drunk. I found her truck. I banged on the back of it but I got the feeling Doug wasn't in there. It has a certain kind of echo when it's empty.'

'So,' Ray inspected the palms of his hands, 'either she dumped him somewhere or she took him to hospital . . .'

'Or else . . .'

'What?'

'Or else she never took him in the first place.'

Ray didn't seem impressed by this line of reasoning. He said, 'Then why would she have taken her truck and gone and got herself so drunk that she could hardly string a sentence together?'

I shook my head. 'I don't know. Maybe she was ashamed. She wrecked the greenhouse. I'm positive of that.'

'And maybe,' Ray added, catching on to the whys and wherefores of speculation, 'maybe Saleem did tell Doug after all, after she'd promised not to, about Nancy being blind in her eye.'

It was feasible, but I couldn't help wondering what Saleem would have to gain from that particular line of action. I told Ray as much. Ray stared at me, wide-eyed.

'You, of course,' he said.

'Me?'

'She likes you.'

'Nancy likes *me*?'

Ray cackled at this. When he laughed he tensed his belly and his night-shirt lifted to reveal the top of his dimpled knees. 'Not Nancy, Saleem!'

'Saleem?'

'Yep.'

My chin dropped. 'You don't know that.'

'I know it.'

'She hates me.'

'She hates everybody, but she hates you with a special kind of, uh, intensity.' Ray was proud of these four fancy syllables. He would have worn them on his lapel as a badge if it had been possible.

I said, 'I think that just means that she hates me more than other people, not that she . . .' I couldn't say it, no way. 'Not that she . . . hates me any less.'

Ray shrugged. 'I didn't mean to step over the mark,' he said, 'I just thought it might have had something to do with this particular situation.'

He nodded over towards Nancy. 'She thinks you don't like her,' he added, off the top of his head.

'Nancy?'

'No! Saleem!' He laughed.

'She thinks I don't like her? Why would she think that?'

'I don't know. She just does.'

'How do you know?'

'Just little things.'

'Like what?'

'Well . . .' Ray thought about it for a while, 'she thinks she makes you angry. You never pay her any attention when she talks to you. You just get, kind of, huffy.'

'Huffy?'

'Yeah.'

I scratched my head. Why was I having this conversation? It was so embarrassing and I was embracing that embarrassment, but Ray plainly didn't know what he was talking about.

'Maybe we should phone Mercy,' Ray said, changing tack suddenly, 'and see if Doug's there. Or maybe I should ring around some of the hospitals in the area and see if he's been checked in.'

'We wouldn't want to ring Mercy and make her worry unnecessarily,' I said, and then realized that Saleem had said the very same thing earlier that afternoon. 'I'm sure Doug's capable of looking after himself. I don't think Nancy could have done anything too terrible to him. We'll just have to wait until she sobers up a bit and see what she says then.'

'And what about the meeting?'

'Hopefully Doug will have turned up by the morning.'

'And what if he's crackers?'

'We'll work something out.'

Nancy started snoring. Her mouth vibrated into the pillow.

'She's got her own built-in muffler, there,' Ray said, smiling, and added, 'By the way, I don't think she's a bad person at heart. I don't think she'd've wrecked the greenhouse without someone else putting her up to it.'

'Well, I didn't,' I said, somewhat stupidly.

'Neither did I,' Ray said quickly. 'And Doug wouldn't have. And the Chinaman . . .'

'Forget about him.'

'Yeah.'

We stared at each other in silence for a moment, then Ray showed me out.

RAY LIVES ON a strange street. Actually it's a road, Avondale Road, and his flat is next door to the house where Stevie Smith, the poet, used to live. I checked my watch. Eleven twenty-two. Now what?

Stevie Smith, as far as I know, was Palmers Green's most famous inhabitant, ever. The house she had lived in – a plain and undistinguished place – was rendered exceptional only by the cobalt-blue plaque on its wall. I stared at the plaque but it was too dark to read it properly.

And I didn't know much about Stevie except that she lived with her aunt and dressed like a little girl when she was old and that she drank a bit too much because she was lonely, sometimes. And one other thing: she was loyal. She had lived in Palmers Green her whole life. On this street. Sometimes she went riding in the parks, or walking in them. And she had loved this place; strange, lonely old Stevie, she had loved this place, just like I do. Just like Doug does. Just like Ray and Nancy. Just like Saleem.

'Where's Doug?'

Saleem had Cog under her arm. She didn't look like she was expecting me. She was wearing a dirty vest and some cut-off jeans. 'What the fuck are you doing here?'

'I saw the light was on.'

'So?' She held Cog under her arm like he was a hot water bottle.

'Doug. Where is he? Do you know where he is? Is he inside? Is he upstairs?'

'What kind of a stupid question is that? Nancy's got him. I already told you.'

'I've seen Nancy. He wasn't with her.'

'What did she tell you?'

'Nothing. She was drunk.'

Saleem licked her lips. 'She's such a slut. She deserved to be fired.'

'That's not what you were saying earlier.'

'Maybe I changed my mind. It's a woman's prerogative.'

'Did you tell Doug?'

'What?'

'About Nancy's eye.'

'Of course not. But I'll certainly consider telling him if you don't go to that meeting tomorrow.'

'No,' I said, 'you won't tell Doug.'

Saleem tightened her grip on Cog, who had started to writhe and to wriggle. Her arm was a vice around his midriff. When she tightened her grip, a little squeak of protest shot out of him.

'Why not?' Saleem asked, slitting her eyes. 'Nancy's expendable.'

'I'll tell you why not. If you tell Doug about Nancy's eye, I'll tell Doug about the fact that you burned the museum down. I'll tell Doug and anyone else who'll listen that it was arson, not an accident after all.'

'I don't think you'd do that.'

'Try me.'

Saleem was silent for a minute and then she said, 'Actually, why don't you come in for a while? We should talk this over. I've only just brewed some tea.'

She pulled the door wide. I hesitated. 'Look,' she said, suddenly, 'of course I wouldn't tell Doug about Nancy. I'm just trying to make sure that you'll go tomorrow, that's all. I have no real problem with Nancy. See?'

Maybe she knew I wasn't keen to come in. She turned and let go of the front door so that I had to catch it to stop it from closing in my face and by the time I'd pushed it wide again she had already disappeared into the kitchen. I closed the door behind me and followed her in. She was holding two cups full of steaming tea. She offered me one. 'Herbal,' she said, 'peppermint. Sit down.'

I sat down. Saleem took a sip of her tea. 'I suppose you saw the maze,' she said, 'in among the receipts and things.'

'Yes.'

'He ordered all that privet and he hasn't even got planning permission. He knows full well that they'd refuse. I don't think we could accuse Enfield Borough of being all that imaginative.'

'I suppose not.' I sipped my tea. It was horrible. Too strong and not peppermint. Fennel, more like.

'I must say,' she added, pulling out a chair for herself, 'I'm very impressed by your loyalty to Nancy. Very impressed.' She fixed me in her steely gaze and smiled. I drank some more tea. I looked down into my cup and then drank more still.

Breathe one, I thought. Breathe two. Breath three.

'I wonder,' Saleem said, then didn't add anything. I wondered what Saleem was wondering but I didn't ask because I was certain that it would be something bad or something cruel. My tea was hot but I drained my cup and put it down decisively.

'Right,' I said, but didn't stand up like I'd intended to.

'I wonder,' Saleem said again, reaching down to stroke Cog, 'I wonder whether you actually *would* tell Doug about the museum. I mean, it's not as though they could prove anything, really. It was so long ago.' She smiled. 'And I was so very, very careful.'

She was still stroking the cat, so I chanced it. 'You lost your leg,' I said, 'you couldn't have been that careful.'

She ignored me. 'I'm not at all intimidated,' she said, 'by your little threat to tell on me. Not at all. I'm only interested in whether you would tell.' She straightened up and stared at me, then added, eventually, 'And I actually think you would, too.'

My mouth went dry. I said, 'Nancy's tough, but she can't defend herself against someone like you.'

Saleem shrugged. 'There's no need for her to defend herself. I have nothing against Nancy. This is between you and me.'

I yawned. It seemed such an inappropriate response to what she was saying, but I simply couldn't help myself.

'Hope I'm not boring you.'

I yawned again. My mouth felt drier still.

'I don't know why,' Saleem said, very quietly it seemed, 'but I always think that when you confide in a person, when you give them a present of something private that's hidden away in your heart, well, then that's like a kind of bond between you, a link. And if someone threatens to break that bond . . .' She whistled under her breath. 'What could be worse than that, Phil? What crime could be worse than that?'

I would have answered, I had plenty to say on this matter and on other related matters, too, but when I tried to move my mouth it wouldn't move. I stared at Saleem for a little while. She stared back at me. Then my head fell slowly forward on to the table. I stared at the grain in the tablecloth for a long, long time. It was the oddest sensation, seeing the rest of Thursday trickle away and sensing Saleem moving around in the kitchen like a dark, hard, sharp arachnid.

Friday

FIRST THING I remember: a musky, dusky, single-limbed bundle of badness was sitting on my lap with a razor. I couldn't do anything. Had I been asleep? I guessed I must've been. I felt very heavy. Could've been her weight on me.

'Hello Phil,' she said, when I opened my eyes, and then carried on touching my skin with the blade.

'Usually,' she said, 'I use this razor under my arms. See?' She lifted her arm. I saw the pores under her armpit, close up like little craters. 'Nearly finished,' she sighed, lowering her arm and wiping off a spot of foam from the blade and on to the vest she was wearing. 'Hot,' she said, 'isn't it?'

I wondered how long we'd been having this conversation. Might've been hours.

'There!' Saleem threw the razor on to the table and dried her hands on her vest, then lifted up the front of the vest and rubbed my face with it. I sensed her breasts against my shoulder. I couldn't feel them, but I sensed them, soft. Soft.

When she'd finished wiping me she pulled back for a moment and stared. 'You know, you're quite a dandy, really.'

I stared back, blankly.

She shifted on my lap, sat sideways, one leg dangling down, the other, truncated, stiff and horizontal like the erect, docked tail of a pointer.

'It's nice,' she said, casually, 'to have a bit of company.'

'Feel this?' she asked, a moment later. I felt nothing. I tried to shake my head. I blinked.

'What's that mean? Yes? No? Feel this?' she asked again. I stared straight ahead. I felt nothing.

'Only,' she said, slightly preoccupied, 'you've got an erection. Either that or . . .' She shifted on my lap. 'Either that or you've got the keys to the main gates in your pocket. Do you happen to know off-hand if you have those on you?'

I tried to nod, couldn't.

'The ones with the big, wooden . . .' she guffawed, 'the big, wooden key-ring? Hang on.'

She dug her hands into my pockets. She removed some small change, an old tartan handkerchief, a couple of till receipts.

'No keys,' she said, smiling. From the other pocket she removed my wallet. She opened it, looked inside and, finding nothing of interest, tossed it down on to the table. 'Right,' she said, 'do you want me to kiss you?'

I remained frozen. She moved up close to my face. Her arms wound around me. She closed her eyes and caught my top lip between her teeth, then let go with her teeth and held my lip between her two lips. Her breath tasted of germoline and bubblegum. Sweet and antiseptic.

She opened her eyes. 'Your face,' she said, 'is very swollen. You look like an apple that's been peeled and soaked in water. Kind of bloated.'

She licked my cheek like a cat with a tight tongue. In my ear she whispered, 'Why do you hate me? What did I ever do? You evil son of a fucking bitch.'

She unwound an arm from around my neck. 'I'm undoing your trousers.' More wriggling. 'I've taken off my knickers. See?' She held a pair of old, skinny black flannel briefs in front of me, then dropped them. 'Apparently,' she grinned, turning to face me, 'you're drugged and heavy and dumb and kind of numb, but one tiny little part of you is still awake, has a mind and a motivation all of its own. Life's a killer like that,' she added, 'isn't it? Full of those wicked, bitter, little surprises.'

She pulled off her vest. I could see her shoulders and her shoulder-blades. My mind was caught up in a debate with itself about whether I would like to be feeling something or whether I preferred not to feel. I could not feel. I could not.

Saleem kissed my lips again. 'That's right,' she muttered, 'move your hands just that way.'

My hands? What was I missing?

'I'm kidding you,' she smirked. 'Your hands aren't moving.'

Her face, close up, seemed damp. When I listened, I could hear a pan boiling on the oven and the air was full of steam. Saleem nudged my cheek with her nose. 'One moment,' she whispered, and pulled herself up, both her hands pushing on my shoulders, and then one hand let go, for a second, before she lowered herself down again, but slowly this time, her face puckering with something like spite but not quite. She sighed. 'This is a good kind,' she whispered, 'a sweet kind of revenge.'

I wished I could feel something. Anything. Only my eyes and my lips. She kissed my lips and then sucked the air out of me. She rose and she fell. The simplest, the slightest of movements: she was a small lake, lapping away in her own time, rolling and riding with her own regular momentum. Gentle waves, rising, falling. Tiny sighs like gusts on the water.

The chair was rocking. I stared at her face. Her eyes were closed. She was smiling. She had nice teeth. I hadn't noticed before what good teeth she had. She leaned back a bit. If I looked down I could see her breasts. I looked up again. I looked down again. What could I feel? A tingling in my chin and in my neck.

She leaned in closer and bit the side of my throat with her fine teeth. I could feel it. I felt something. Her hair tangled around my ears. Her hands touched my shoulders, lightly, and then my chest. She pulled at the buttons on my shirt. I could feel my shoulders, and just below, I was sure I felt something.

While she undid my buttons she whispered into my ears. 'Is this hurting? As bad as I want it to? You evil, loyal, Nancy-loving little fuck.' She pulled her head around and stared into my eyes. 'Is it?'

I was sure I could have answered, but I remained as stiff as if I couldn't answer. I could feel my ribs and my belly. I could feel them. She pushed her hands down on to my hips. I felt her hands. They prickled on me like itchy peaches.

Her breathing quickened. She rose and she fell. I could feel my belly. I could feel below my belly. Oh, I wanted to feel her so badly! Her eyes were closed and if I shifted my neck slightly I could see her breasts which were lifting as she was breathing, and shimmering wetly. I watched as a drop of perspiration swooped and shot from her chin to her stomach. I wanted to catch it on my lip.

Her eyes were still shut as she pushed herself up close. I could feel her so softly against me. She kissed my lips and she was smiling when she drew away, and she was very glisteny as she pulled back and as she opened her eyes.

I could feel something. Oh Christ! Something dark and strong and hot and tight and urgent as anything. The chair was still rocking. I could feel something.

She froze. She was glaring, all of a sudden. She stared at me. She had stopped moving. 'It's no fucking good,' she said, savagely. 'Fucking Nancy! Nancy! I don't believe it. You'd fuck me over just for Nancy. That bitch. Fuck it.' She pushed herself up. Oh, that was too bad. That was too, too bad. 'Fuck Nancy! Fuck her! Fuck you! Fuck you both.'

She hopped over to the oven, picked up a saucepan, hit herself hard on the side of her head with it.

'Ow!' she yelled, staggering, and then hitting the table, gathering speed, all the time, until, finally, with the swiftest and the smartest backhand I'd ever witnessed, she hit me. *Bop.*

I WAS GOING to stay quiet this time. I was going to give no indication – absolutely none – that I was awake. The lights were off, which was a good sign. I was lying on the kitchen floor, slightly curved, arched like a banana with my head resting on the bunched up tablecloth and with Cog looped around me, like a fur muffler across my neck.

If I looked up I could see through the blind. The sky was lighter than pure dark. 3 a.m.? 4 a.m.? I held my breath to see if I could hear anything. Cog's stomach rumbled and then he yawned. I slowly raised my arm and lifted him off me.

I sat up. My foot touched something metallic which shifted and clattered. I froze. I squinted. It was the saucepan that Saleem had hit me with. I put the hand to the side of my head. My head felt odd. My whole face felt odd. I rubbed my hands up and down it and it was like someone else's face. Soft and bare and rubbery. Altogether different.

I turned my mind back. I touched my face again. I almost panicked. Who was I? It was dark. Who was I? I stood up. I looked around me. I had to see myself.

Everything ached. Into the hallway. Up the stairs. I needed a mirror. The bathroom was the first door to the left on the landing. I pushed the door wide and slid inside. I closed the door and switched on the light. I blinked. Oh my Christ.

My face was bare and clean and neat as a cauliflower. Bruised florets above my eye and on my cheek. My eyebrows had gone. My hairline had been cut back by three inches so that I looked like a Franciscan monk or Henry VIII or Coco the Clown in a wind tunnel.

I was so angry. Saleem had wanted me to go to the meeting and I had been coming round to the idea, I had been seriously considering it, actually contemplating it – I told myself, I believed myself – and now this. How could I go looking this way? Had she no faith in me? I was angry. It was a stupid feeling. I was angry as hell.

Where was she? I tried the first door to my left. An empty

113

room. Second door. A cupboard. Third door. Shower unit. The right-hand side. The first door. I pushed it open.

Doug. It was dark and Doug was darker but I saw him, lying on a double bed, arm hanging off the side of it, mouth open, eyes open, staring up at the ceiling. I almost withdrew but something stopped me.

'Doug?'

He didn't move.

'Doug?'

I stepped up closer. One step, two steps. Closer still. I stood over him.

'Doug?'

I touched his shoulder. He felt cold. I looked into his eyes. They didn't focus.

'Doug?'

I touched his cheek. Waxy. I put my hand next to his mouth. No air. I pulled the blanket up to his chin. I shuddered.

'Doug?'

I backed out of the room, quietly, slowly.

The next door along. I tried it. Saleem's room. She was on her bed too, curled up like a squirrel under the sheets. I opened my mouth to say her name but I didn't say anything. I squatted down next to her. The side of her face was bruised where she'd hit herself. Her bottom lip stuck out like she was sulking with sleep.

I leaned forward, barely breathing, and I don't know what I was planning to do. Maybe I was intending to get right up close to her ear and then to shout in it, to scare her, to start to pay her back for all the bad things she'd done. Perhaps not.

In fact I drew close and I found myself touching her cheek with the tips of my fingers. She opened her eyes. 'Climb in,' she said, dopily. 'Come on.'

I pulled off my shirt. I pulled off my trousers. I pulled up the sheet and climbed in. Under the sheet she was as warm as baked bread. She curled around me and pressed her nose to my neck. I touched her hair with one hand. With the other I touched her hip and her thigh and her left breast which was like moss only softer. She crawled around me, like I was an old sofa and she was settling herself comfortably.

She kissed me. I kissed her. I counted the bumps on her spine with my index finger, pushing the skin on her back and feeling it slide. She took hold of my hand and guided it down, between her legs, and then lower, to her lost leg, to where it stopped. The scar tissue had left it as fragile as a petal. Just like a plant, I thought, when it's been pruned back in autumn. And I drew my hand up her leg again. And I kissed her.

'Fuck Nancy.' I said, feeling her moving.

'Fuck me,' she said, and almost started laughing. And I would have, but I kept thinking about Doug and whether I'd dreamed him.

'Doug's dead,' I said, finding a place to fit myself.

'He's not dead,' she sighed, 'only sleeping.'

'I don't think so,' I sighed back. 'He isn't breathing.'

'What?'

I said nothing. I carried on moving.

'What?'

She pushed me off and sat up. 'Why the hell didn't you tell me before?'

The light shone down brightly and rudely. Saleem was wearing my shirt. I wore my trousers, hastily pulled on. I buttoned up the fly as I watched her.

'Oh God,' she said, 'you're right. He doesn't seem to be breathing. Can you feel a pulse? Do you know where to look for one?'

I drew closer to the bed. 'His eyes. Open like that,' I said, squeamishly, 'that's what struck me as wrong, first off.'

'His pulse!' she yelled furiously, 'where is it?'

I grabbed hold of Doug's wrist. I stuck my thumb across it and pressed down hard.

'I don't feel anything,' I said, 'but I'm probably not doing it right. What did you give him?'

'Same stuff you had.'

She was slapping his face now, gently and then harder.

'What stuff?'

'Tea, stupid.'

'Tea? Where from?'

'I made it. Boiled it.'

'Boiled what?'

'You know, that stuff. You told me about it.'

'Stop hitting him. If he's dead it won't be helping matters. If he comes to, he'll be livid.'

She turned and glared, 'D'you have any better suggestions?'

'What kind of tea was it?'

'I can't remember the name. You pointed it out to me. You told me to boil the root.'

Things started slotting into place.

'A plant? And you gave it to me too?'

She grunted her affirmation. She had her ear next to Doug's lips.

'Why did you give it to me?'

'You fucked me off. It was only temper. I regret it in retrospect.'

'I could've been dead too.'

'You only had a cupful.'

'What did Doug have?'

'Since this morning? Two pints.'

'How did you get him to drink it?'

'Told him the first lot was brandy. He knocked it straight back. Second lot I fed him through a straw.'

'Maybe he choked. You shouldn't have done that.'

Saleem looked up at me. 'What shall we do if we've killed him?'

'We? We've killed him? I haven't been anywhere near him.'

Her mouth turned down at its corners. 'Great one. Who was it told me about the plant? You did. I wouldn't mind, but you came in here, saw Doug was distressed and your only course of action was to creep into my room to try and cop off with me. That in itself is tantamount to bloody manslaughter.'

I stared back at her. 'You are truly a vixen,' I said, stunned.

Her face slowly crumpled, as readily as a fistful of tissue paper. She flung herself across Doug's chest. 'Oh Christ!' she said, 'and I really love Doug.'

I went and sat down on the other side of the bed. I said, 'I didn't know you loved Doug.'

'Of course I do,' she muttered, through tears and through mucus. 'Why else would I have gone to all this trouble?'

'For yourself,' I said.

She pulled her head up and stared at me. 'To think,' she said, 'to think I was going to let you fuck me. My God.'

I stared back at her. 'You poisoned me, you lied to me, you shaved my eyebrows off, you hit me with a saucepan.'

Saleem sniffed. She appraised me. She said, 'You have such a negative approach to things.'

'Where did you get the plant from?'

'Inside the museum. The plant which grew from my leg. I thought it was a sign.'

'The grenadilla.'

'The passion flower.' She nodded.

'Didn't you stop and think about how strong the stuff was? After you boiled it?'

'Of course I did,' she scowled. 'I tried it out on the cat.'

'The cat.' I smiled.

'What are you smiling at?'

'The cat,' I said. 'Remember?'

'What?' She was losing her temper again.

'You thought you'd killed the cat.'

'So?'

I decided to tell her. 'OK,' I said, 'I'll admit it. I felt Doug's pulse. And he blinked.'

'What?'

'While you were sobbing just now he blinked.'

Her eyes were round as two full moons. 'He blinked? He blinked, you fucker, and you didn't tell me?' She lunged at me. I stood up. I was very proud of myself, suddenly. I was avenged.

Saleem was looking around her for some kind of weapon.

'Let's hope,' I said quickly, 'that Doug comes to in time for the meeting.'

Saleem had grabbed hold of the bedside light and was trying to yank the plug out of the wall by its cord. It wouldn't come, thankfully.

'Doug's not dead,' I said, resolutely, 'which is something to be pleased about, surely.' She stopped yanking for a moment. 'And you love Doug,' I said, 'apparently, so you should be ecstatic.'

'Get stuffed.'

Saleem put down the lamp and stared into Doug's face. 'He's still out cold,' she said and then peered up at me. 'I knew you wouldn't go to the meeting. I knew it. That's why I got so angry.'

I was indignant. I said, 'I was seriously considering going.'

'Bollocks.'

'Before you shaved my eyebrows off.'

'Bollocks you were. I knew you wouldn't. You don't have the guts.'

I shrugged. There seemed little point responding. I said, 'May I have my shirt back, please?'

'Why?'

'I want to go home now. I'm tired.'

Saleem left the room. I sat down on the bed again and looked at Doug. He was still fast asleep but his eyes remained open. I considered trying to pull down the lids, gently. I leaned over him.

'What are you doing?'

Saleem stood in the doorway, dressed in her vest and some knickers. The sight of her strange, pale stump almost made me smile. There was something so special about it. Something neat and extraordinary. She tossed me my shirt and I pulled it on.

'You won't believe it,' I said, determining to carry on embarrassing myself, if needs be for the rest of my whole stupid life, 'but I love Doug too.'

'You don't.'

'I do.'

'How?'

'What do you mean?'

'How do you love him?'

I shrugged. I said, 'He's great.'

Her eyebrows rose. I added. 'I mean great, like Julius Caesar or someone. Napoleon. A giant personality.'

'I'll tell you what he is,' Saleem said sourly. 'He's an unholy pain in the fucking arse and he's half-mad.'

'I know.' I stared into Doug's dead eyes. 'He's everything.'

'Come downstairs.' She beckoned me from the doorway. 'Why?'

'I can't talk properly in here with Doug lying there.'

I stood up. I followed Saleem to the top of the stairs. She didn't have a stick with her and refused the arm I offered. Instead she sat on the top step and then bumped down on her bottom. I remembered doing just that when I was small. As she bumped down and I followed her, I said, 'How did Nancy get involved in all this?'

'Fucking Nancy,' she grumbled.

'I'm only interested.'

'Christ, you're so pleased with yourself all of a sudden.'

Am I? I wondered. I couldn't think why I should be.

Saleem reached the bottom of the stairs and pulled herself up on the banister. I saw from the rear that her bottom was pink with friction. She hopped into the kitchen. She went and turned on the kettle.

'I'm going to have a boiled egg,' she said, and set about preparing it.

I sat down at the table. The sun was thinking about coming up. My hand was still swollen. My ankle looked horrible, bright and red like the skin might crack and blister.

Saleem pulled out a chair for herself. 'OK,' she said, licking some margarine from her thumb, 'so you think I'm a shit. And yes, I did kind of twist Nancy's arm. The point is, though,' she turned as the kettle boiled but didn't move to make some tea. I stood up instead and made some coffee.

'The point is, right, when I heard about Nancy's eye from

119

Ray it seemed like too good an opportunity to miss. Shall I tell you why?'

'Why?'

'Because it's all just crap. Ray might've noticed about Nancy's eye before the rest of us, but what he doesn't realize is that Nancy's perfectly within her rights to drive with only one eye.'

'How do you know that?'

'I thought it best to find out the details before I set about blackmailing her. I phoned the Department of Transport.'

Saleem smirked. 'And I'll tell you something else. If you check out the damage on the truck and the receipts for the repairs on the other accidents she's had, it turns out that all the smashes were on the *left* hand side of the truck.'

'What does that mean?'

'She's over-compensating, stupid. Her eye isn't the problem at all. The problem is that she's so het-up about the eye that she's driving badly by trying to overcompensate for it. She's so paranoid about the possibility of losing her job that she didn't even think to find out whether it was ever a problem in the first place.'

'So it isn't?'

'Nope.'

'But you blackmailed her anyway.'

'Yep. I needed her to help me carry Doug's body upstairs, and as a decoy.' She stared at me, unrepentant. 'I told her we'd all lose everything if Doug wasn't stopped from going to the meeting. I also threatened to tell you about her eye and how she'd deceived you. I convinced her and I convinced Ray that you were a man of integrity. I told them you'd stand by Doug come hell or high water, if you believed he was in the right. Even if he was mad.'

I passed her a mug of coffee. She took the mug. 'Thanks.'

'So all of this,' I said nervously, 'has been for my benefit.'

'Yep. To prove to you that Doug was mad; you needed irrefutable proof. To corner you, to bully you, to beguile you.'

She took a gulp of her coffee and then hopped over to the oven to remove her egg. She put it on to a saucer and then hopped back to the table. She knocked it on the saucer and then started to peel it.

'I realized, though,' she said, preoccupied with the egg, 'when I left you this afternoon, that you had no intention of going to the meeting.'

'Why?'

'Why? Because you don't really love Doug. You don't understand Doug.'

'How can you say that?'

The egg was peeled now. 'How? Because if you loved Doug you'd want to go to the meeting. You'd want to help him. You wouldn't think that all the things I'd done to him were bad. You'd understand that I'm Doug's friend and so I want to protect him.'

I almost laughed at this. Saleem ignored me and took a bite of her egg.

'You think you're different,' she said, chewing and swallowing, 'but you aren't different at all, you only feel different on the inside. But me and Doug, we just can't help it. People think we're different because we are, physically. We're a different colour. Doesn't matter how much you do. It doesn't fucking matter how much you care. You won't fit. People won't let you. Even if you find the most perfect landscape and it's yours. Even then.'

I stared at her, flummoxed.

'You're a part of this place,' she said. 'No one doubts it.'

'Doug's a part of it too. So are you.'

She carried on eating her egg in silence. Eventually she said, 'How you feel and fact, Phil. Two entirely different matters.'

I tried to work out which was worse: feeling different but fitting in or being different but feeling in your heart like you should fit but not quite fitting. Which was worse? Stupid question.

Saleem finished her egg. She sucked her fingers clean. I stared at her. 'Would you have told on Nancy?' I asked, eventually.

She shrugged. 'Dunno. I like to think I'm capable of anything.' She licked her lips and added, 'We're back to Nancy again, I see.'

'No,' I said, 'I was only thinking about what you were saying earlier, before you drugged me.'

'What was I saying?'

'About how you have a responsibility to someone once you know their secrets.'

She sighed, 'Screw it. We're going to lose everything anyway.'

'You really think so?'

'I know it.'

'Where will you go?'

'Who cares? This is the only place I fit.'

'And Doug?'

'He's everything, he's everywhere. Poor fucker.'

We sat in silence for a while. 'OK,' I said, 'I'll go to the meeting. I don't know why I made such a fuss about going in the first place.'

I thought of my funeral suit, hanging up in my wardrobe. My heart contracted.

'We've got nothing to lose,' I added, thinking, at the same time, about the herb garden and the ornamental pond, the ducks, the geese.

'I'll wait and see,' Saleem said, showing a laudable lack of faith in me. 'I'll believe you've actually gone only when I see it with these two eyes.'

She pointed. We were both silent for a while. Upstairs I could hear Cog walking down the passageway. Saleem looked up at the ceiling.

'The cat,' I said.

She shook her head, 'He's on my lap.'

'Doug!' I exclaimed, feeling something slither down my spine.

We both listened. Doug was dragging himself up the corridor and into the bathroom.

'What time is it?'

Saleem knocked the cat off her lap, leaned back on her chair and stared at the clock on the cooker. 'Six fifteen.'

'When's the meeting?'

'Nine sharp.'

Upstairs I heard the taps turning.

'What's he doing?'

'Having a wash. Maybe a bath. He usually gets up at about this time. Just shows you. He was comatose an hour ago. He's so bloody determined. That's what happens when your mind starts to turn.'

I was suddenly frightened. I said, guiltily, 'I don't suppose you could give him some more tea?'

She shook her head. 'I'm not risking it.' She smiled at me. 'So now what, Phil? Any suggestions?'

My head was empty.

'There's a heavy chest of drawers,' she said, softly, 'in my bedroom. You could push it up against the bathroom door. Jam him in.'

My heart began beating. 'I'm very weak,' I said, nervously. 'My hand and my foot.'

'It's up to you.'

'He'll go mad.'

'He's mad already. It'll only be like more of the same. And anyway,' she added, 'he'll still be kind of slow and fuzzy, like you were when you first woke up.'

I remembered and began blushing. 'Fine,' I said.

The drawers were heavy. I couldn't get any grip with my bad hand and I couldn't get any thrust with my bad foot. After five minutes I'd got them to the doorway of Saleem's room. I paused a moment to get my breath back. While I paused the bathroom door – directly opposite – opened and out came Doug, still steaming from his bath and wrapped in a towel. He looked lidded and dopy. He paused in the hallway and appraised me.

'Phil,' he said, eventually, groping for my name. *Feel.*

I froze. My heart stopped and then it started up again. 'Hi Doug.'

He stared at the chest of drawers. 'What's going on?'

'Nothing. I'm helping Saleem move some furniture.'

'You look different,' he mumbled and scratched his head, like he couldn't quite believe he wasn't just imagining me. I took a deep breath.

'Actually,' I said, thinking on my feet, speaking quickly, 'I think you cut yourself shaving. On your cheek. It's bleeding.'

'Yeah?' Doug put his hand to his cheek, blinking with the effort this afforded him.

'You'd better go and check in the mirror.'

Doug slowly turned and went back into the bathroom.

'Is it bad?' I asked, 'It might've just been a nick.'

Doug didn't reply straight off. I bounded over the drawers, pushed the bathroom door to, bounced back again and gave them a mighty shove. A deep breath and then another shove. During the second shove Doug tried to open the door but the door only pushed ajar by five inches before I gave the drawers a third great heave and knocked it shut.

I waited for a minute, in silence, breathing heavily, sweating. After a minute, Doug said, 'Phil, I have a beard. I haven't shaved with a razor in fifteen years.' His voice sounded muffled through the wood. Thick-grained and oaky. He tried the door. Another minute. 'Phil,' he said, 'what's the problem?' I felt my heart swoop. Doug tried the door again, more aggressively this time.

With impeccable timing, Saleem appeared at the end of the corridor. She put her finger to her lips. I realized my mouth was open. What had I been intending to say? I closed it. She slid past me and into her room then came out dragging an old camp bed. She put her lips next to my ear and whispered, 'If we prop this between the drawers and the wall there's no way he'll be able to get the door open.'

I took hold of the bed and did as she'd said. Doug was silent for a moment. I guessed he was intent on listening for any noises outside. Then I heard him curse under his breath before he launched a full-blown attack on the door. The door shook. I stepped back, shocked by his sudden vigour.

'It'll hold,' Saleem whispered, apparently unfazed. 'It's an old house. The doors are solid and so are the frames.'

She grabbed my hand and pulled me away to the top of the stairs. Doug was still raging in that small, square room with all the conviction of a wild boar in a balsa-wood crate.

'Ignore him,' Saleem said, calmly, 'Here's the plan. You go home now and get yourself something to eat and have a wash. Get changed into your suit. Catch the number 29 bus into Enfield. The Council offices are a short walk from the market place. You've been there before, haven't you? You know the address?'

I nodded.

'Good. Get there for nine and don't be late. Tell them that Doug's got flu and we didn't want to cancel again. Tell them you've got a roundworm and that's why you've lost some hair and your face is such a mess. Bullshit them about the privet. Don't forget the files and the accounts.'

Doug was still banging against the door and yelling now.

'What if I screw up?'

She grinned. 'If you screw up, I'll tell Doug that you locked him in there on purpose. When he gets out he'll hunt you down and kill you.'

'He knows I locked him in there,' I said, trembling. 'He came out while I was shifting the drawers and I had to speak to him. He *knows* I locked him in. Oh Christ,' I said desperately, 'why did I do it?'

Saleem's grin slipped for a moment and then rose up again and regained control of her face. 'We'll tell him he dreamed it. I'll say I was moving my room around and halfway through I went out to buy a bottle of furniture polish so I didn't hear him yelling.'

'D'you think that'll work?'

'No. Sod him, though. Keeping this place going is our top priority.'

I stared at her, sweating and frantic and suddenly suspicious. I said, 'I thought we were doing this for Doug.'

Saleem scowled. 'We have a whole series of priorities, Phil. Like a set of balls which you have to keep juggling. You can only keep a certain number in the air at any one time.'

Doug was baying at the bathroom door. It sounded like he was biting at the paintwork. I was frightened.

'And afterwards,' I said, terrified, 'who's going to let him out of there?'

Saleem sniffed, put her head to one side, thought for a moment. 'We'll toss for it. Now fuck off.'

BY RIGHTS I should have expected him, but it still came as a surprise to come across him standing on one small foot next to the giant yellow broom. Wu. I wished he'd stay in one place and then I could have been sure to avoid that area. A quiet corner where no one would see him and he, in turn, could see no one.

He was in his own world. I stood, out of sight, behind a silver birch, and I watched him. Just like Doug had. He was so beautiful. I couldn't help myself. Doug was right, of course. He was so much a part of the landscape. Taking what he wanted from his surroundings. Digesting the good things, rejecting the bad things. A part of the universe and yet entirely himself. Flowing. Needing nothing, owning everything.

Was that what Doug craved? Was that what I wanted? And Saleem? I didn't think so. We were all smaller. Wanted to hold something. A small space. A small holding. And the smaller the holding, the harder to hold. The smaller, the harder.

I slipped my arms around the tree and clung to it, until it was time to let go.

MY FUNERAL SUIT. The files. Enfield. An office. Four men and me.

It was hard, to start off with, so instead of evading and avoiding – my normal course of action – I embarrassed myself on purpose. Straight away. Up front. I gave myself a proper reason. I said, 'Sorry about the way I look. I developed an allergy to a new type of weedkiller we're using.'

They stared at me, smiled, and then they stopped staring.

'I'm sorry Doug couldn't make it,' I added. 'I'm a poor second best but he has the flu and didn't want to risk spreading it.'

Two of them nodded, the third one stared out of the window (in a world of his own), the fourth was inspecting the files.

'Things have been tight,' I said, preparing to mention the deficit, to discuss the privet, the insurance.

'Actually,' the man with the folder looked up, 'actually, Phil, there's something we need to talk about.'

My heart sank and then, miraculously, it rallied. I resolved, that instant, in a flash of fizzy sweetness, of white-blindness, to tell them about Doug's maze. To tell them. Was it insanity? Doug's crazy plan. I owed him, I decided.

I opened my mouth to speak but someone else spoke first.

'We've had an idea,' the second man said, 'and we aren't sure how you'll take to it, or Doug either for that matter.'

I wanted to tell them so badly. I needed to tell them. I wanted them to see how beautiful Doug's vision was, how complete.

'Crazy golf,' the first man said, and then nudged the third man who was still looking out of the window.

'Crazy golf,' the third man parroted, 'Nine holes. Nothing too big. Family fun and all that.'

The fourth man closed the folder. 'Crazy golf,' he said. 'That's what we've been planning.'

He unfolded a detailed map of the park and laid it out on the table in front of me. He opened up my heart on the table and performed careless surgery on it with the tip of his pencil. 'Right there,' he pointed, 'in that little gap. What do you think?'

HERE'S THE STRANGE PART. I felt odd before, like I was weird and my weirdness was an awful secret just waiting to be discovered. And yet now that I was actually weird – shaved and hairless, bald and bare – now that I was actually weird I found that I didn't really care. No point thinking about it. I was that thing I'd most dreaded being. I was that thing. And frankly, it didn't matter. Not an iota.

I climbed off the bus and walked down Green Lanes, took a right turn on to Aldermans Hill, took a left through the park gates. I was home. I looked around me. What did I see?

I saw litter, I saw weeds, I saw dogshit. If I squinted, in the distance, I could see the crazy golf course. It was there already. Families putting, children dripping their cornets on to the artificial turf, the rubber flooring a bright synthetic colour. I could see it already, a clot in the centre of this little green heart.

I walked towards the house. On the way I passed Ray, securing some climbing roses on to their trellis. He didn't see me. I walked on further and I saw Nancy. She was reversing her truck into the courtyard, her face drawn-up and hung-over. She didn't see me. I turned and headed up the steps, pushed open the door, walked inside the house, into the kitchen.

Doug sat at the kitchen table cradling a mug of Lemsip between his two hands. We stared at each other. I shrivelled.

'Don't ask me,' he said, finally, his voice as deep as the lowest note on a fine, French horn, 'don't ask me how I got here.'

I said nothing. I didn't dare ask.

'So, Phil,' he said, quite affable, 'you went to my meeting.'

I gulped down some air. I nodded.

Doug gazed ruminatively into his mug of Lemsip. 'I suppose,' he said, slowly, 'I suppose I let you down baldie.'

'Pardon?'

He cleared his throat. 'I suppose I let you down badly.'

I put my hand up to my bare face, to my forehead where the hair had been hacked.

'No,' I stuttered, 'You didn't let me down.'

Doug gritted his teeth, 'I should've been there.' He paused. 'I appreciate you stepping in, though. Stepping into the breach. Because things are very *tight* at the moment.' He paused for a second, rubbed his eyes with the back of his hands. 'Very tight,' he repeated.

I nodded stupidly. I'd have agreed to anything. The truth. Lies. 'I know,' I said. Doug pulled his hands away and stared at me.

'Thank you,' he whispered, somewhat gratuitously, and carried on staring. My hackles rose. 'Thank you,' he said again, his voice all honey. My hackles rose even higher. They were ridiculously high, so high I was almost floating, suspended and smarting up close to the ceiling. Doug, I knew, was at his most dangerous when he oozed.

He spread out his hands on to the table.

'You know, life can be a bitch, Phil. And you find yourself tiptoeing through it, barely knowing where to put your feet down, and you hold on to these tiny little things, these tiny little places where you've rested your feet, these spaces. And then sometimes you start to look at these spaces, these places, to really look, and you see how tight they are. Really tight. And you begin to wonder . . .'

I gazed at him, hypnotized.

'How'd that meeting go, Phil?'

'Uh . . . fine.' I couldn't bear to tell him how this space was getting smaller. I couldn't bear to tell him about the nine holes and the artificial turf and the nominal charge and the soft-soled shoes.

'How'd it go, Phil? Did it go well or did it go baldie?'

My hand flew back to my face. 'It went OK, I think.'

'We'll talk about it later, huh?'

I nodded.

Doug's eyes were very gentle, suddenly. I was almost sick with fear. He said, 'I've had the worst head-cold, Phil. And it's been hanging around above my nose for a good while now. And I've been waiting for it to break. Just waiting . . .' Doug paused and stared at me for what seemed like an eternity. 'And then finally it broke.'

I nodded.

'It broke.'

'Right.'

'Still feel rough, though, Phil. Phil?'

'Yes?'

'Still feel rough.'

It was then that I noticed that Doug had a pair of shears on the table, right next to him, and he had been sharpening them. The blades were a bright silver. Doug took hold of the shears. He passed them from one hand to the other. He stood up, still holding them.

'Phil?'

'Yes?'

'Want a cuddle, Phil?'

He was saccharine-voiced. He was smiling. He never smiled, not Doug, not ever. He was going to kill me. I was certain. He would kill me. The shears were sharp enough. I deserved it. He held out his arms. The shears were high and steady in his right hand.

Slowly, stiffly, I approached him. I drew close and then closer. I tucked myself, wincing, into his arms. He chuckled and clucked and then he patted me on the back. He held me.

'The tractor,' he said eventually, 'is it still in the barn?'

I choked as I spoke. 'The tractor? I think so.'

'Good. Good.'

He was as gentle as snow. He squeezed me. I waited for the stab of the blade. He squeezed me again and then let go. Without another word, he drained his Lemsip and then calmly padded out. Out of the kitchen, out of the house.

I was shaking. I took a deep breath and I followed him. Saleem was on the doorstep. She grinned. 'You're pale as pastry. How was he?'

I shuddered, 'I don't really know.'

'And the meeting?'

'The meeting?' I struggled to remember.

The tractor's engine burst into life, its roar reverberated inside the barn. The gears were hacked from neutral and into reverse. Saleem, I realized, was staring up at me. My mind was in the barn. My brain was vibrating.

'You won't shake him, Phil,' she said, gently, 'And you won't shake me.'

What did she mean? She always meant something. She didn't waste words. She was purposeful.

The tractor swung out of the barn, indicated right and then left, straight after.

I said, 'He had some shears on him and I think he picked up a length of hose. Maybe he's thinking about cutting back the big border on the east side.'

'Nah.'

We followed behind at a slow pace. There seemed no reason to rush. As we walked I said, 'You know, I think Doug's right after all about everything going in a circle.'

'Bollocks.'

We walked down and past the burnt-out museum.

'He is right,' I said, growing ever more certain, watching as the tractor turned right and picked up speed.

'Ten pounds,' Saleem whispered, reverently, 'ten pounds says he goes straight into the ornamental pond.'

I put my hand into my pocket. 'Ten pounds he doesn't.'

The tractor veered boldly towards the pond.

'He's my hero,' Saleem said. 'He's off his fucking head.'

And the tractor drew closer to the pond. And the ducks and the geese were waggling their tails and getting nervous. Some stood up. A couple honked and hissed. Doug's hand waved regally from the tractor. He applied his brakes.

'Told you,' I said, cheering up suddenly, forgetting about the crazy golf and the litter and the dog mess and all that other business. 'Told you,' I said, 'he's slowing right down.'

Doug slowed down to a trundle but he didn't stop. Not quite. Instead, very slowly, very carefully, he eased the tractor into the pond: front wheels, back wheels, drove for a few seconds and then stalled.

Saleem showed me the palm of her hand. 'What did I tell you?'

Doug climbed out of the cab, holding his shears and with a length of green hose curled around his arm like a python. He waded through the pond, climbed up and out the other side, turned, waved again, holding the shears aloft, and then carried straight on walking.

Just for an instant, less than a second, Saleem's outstretched palm sagged. 'What's he doing?'

'More to the point,' I said, 'what's he *thinking*?'

'Easy enough,' Saleem smirked, her palm coming back up and flattening out again. 'He's thinking about how badly and how thoroughly he's going to fuck us all over.'

Her face sagged and then it tightened. She cackled. I turned, amazed, and watched her laughing. Then I found myself laughing. She made me laugh. The simple way she sliced through things. The wonderful way that she hissed and she slithered.

And up until that point, I'll admit it, I had been wound up, halted, blocked, but then my mind did something so curious. It flew backwards, it turned, it clicked over – like one of those calendars that each day clicks over a page – and I saw Doug, in that instant, so clearly, so thoroughly.

I saw Doug as many things; pure and bright and full of light. I saw Doug as many things, in all his incarnations; and he was an insect, an egg, a pearl, an onion, a giant onion, many-layered. He was a jewel and a flower and a beautiful, bright yellow bird. He was all these things. He was everything. Doug was God and God was doG and Evil was dEvil and Devil was liveD, was *livid*, red, angry, emergent, emergency, was 999, was 666. I saw them, so clearly. I saw all these things.

And the park was my soul. And I would not leave this place. Soul. Soil. I would not. I could not. I could not leave this place.

It was then that the eye was like the
ear, and the ear like the nose, and the nose like
the mouth: for they were all one and the same.
The mind was in rapture, the form dissolved,
and the bones and flesh all thawed away; and I
did not know how the frame supported itself
and what the feet were treading upon. I gave
myself away to the wind, eastward or west-
ward, like leaves of a tree.

Lieh-tzu